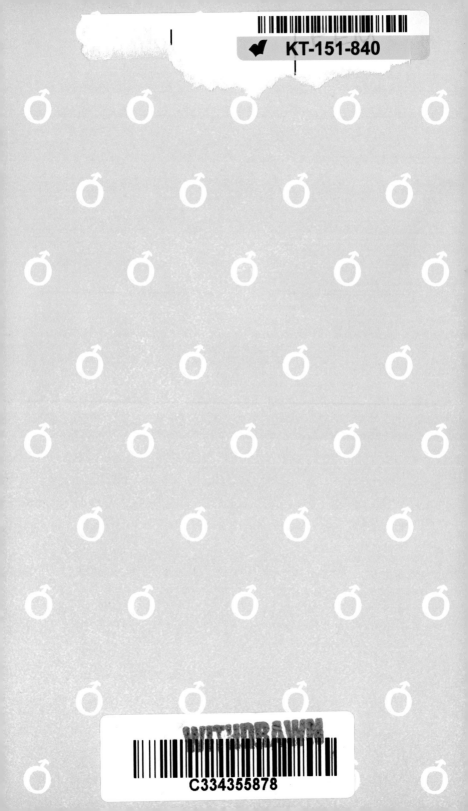

MY BROTHER'S NAME IS JESSICA

PUFFIN BOOKS

UK | USA | Canada | Ireland | Australia
India | New Zealand | South Africa

Puffin Books is part of the Penguin Random House group of companies
whose addresses can be found at global.penguinrandomhouse.com.

www.penguin.co.uk
www.puffin.co.uk
www.ladybird.co.uk

First published 2019

001

Text copyright © John Boyne, 2019

The moral right of the author has been asserted

With thanks to Inclusive Minds and their Inclusion Ambassador
network, in particular Sascha Amel-Kheir, for their input

Set in 11/18 pt Sabon LT Std
Typeset by Jouve (UK), Milton Keynes
Printed and bound in Great Britain by Clays Ltd, Elcograf S.p.A.

A CIP catalogue record for this book is available from the British Library

HARDBACK
ISBN: 978–0–241–37613–3

TRADE PAPERBACK
ISBN: 978–0–241–37615–7

All correspondence to:
Puffin Books
Penguin Random House Children's
80 Strand, London WC2R ORL

MY BROTHER'S NAME IS JESSICA

JOHN BOYNE

PUFFIN

For my nieces, Maya and Ava

1

The Very Strange Afternoon

There's a story I've heard many times about how my brother Jason got the scar that runs above his left eye, almost parallel with his eyebrow. He was four years old when I was born, and he'd wanted a brother, a sister or a dog for as long as he could remember, but Mum and Dad had always said no.

'Nobody needs more than one child,' insisted Dad. 'The planet's overpopulated as it is. Do you know, there's a family in the street next to ours with seven children under the age of six?'

'How is that even possible?' asked my brother Jason, who might have only been a child at the time but knew a little about how the world worked.

'Two sets of twins,' replied Dad with a smile.

'And dogs need constant walking,' added Mum. 'And before you say you'd walk him, we all know that you say that now but, in the end, it'll be your dad or me who ends up doing most of the hard work.'

'But –'

'They create an awful mess too,' said Dad.

'Which?' asked my brother Jason. 'Dogs or siblings?'

'Both.'

Mum and Dad were so insistent that there would be no further additions to our family that it must have come as something of a shock when they sat him down one day to tell him that he was going to get his wish after all and that, in six months' time, there would be a new baby in the house. Apparently, he was so excited he ran out into the back garden and charged around in circles for twenty minutes, screaming at the top of his voice, until he got so dizzy that he fell over and hit his head on a garden gnome.

Although that's not how he got the scar.

When I was born, however, there was a problem. I had a hole in my heart and the doctors didn't think that I was going to survive for very long. The hole was only the size of a pinhead but, when you're a baby and your heart is only the size of a peanut, that can be pretty dangerous. I was kept in an incubator for a few days before being brought to an operating theatre, where a team of surgeons tried to repair what was wrong with me. My brother Jason was at home with the au pair at the time, and cried so hard with worry that he fell off the chair and hit his head on a coffee table.

Although that's not how he got the scar either.

The doctors told my parents that the next week would be critical, but as they've both always had very important jobs – Mum's a Cabinet minister now, although she was just a normal Member of Parliament at the time, and Dad has always been her private secretary – they couldn't be with me constantly and so took it in turns to come to the hospital. Mum came in during the mornings when the House wasn't in session, but she was always being called away for meetings, while Dad arrived during the afternoons but didn't like to stay too long in case there were what he called 'developments' that meant he had to get back to Westminster as quickly as he could. But my brother Jason was brought in to meet me for the first time the night following my operation and, even though he was only four at the time, he refused to go home afterwards, and caused so much trouble that eventually the nurses put a cot in the room next to my incubator and let him stay.

'Baby might sense there's someone here looking out for him,' said the nurse. 'It can't hurt.'

'And at least we know he's safe here,' said Mum.

'Plus, we won't have to pay the au pair double time,' added Dad.

But then, a few nights later, a noise sounded from one of the machines that were keeping me alive and it gave him such a shock that he stumbled out of his cot in search of a doctor, but, as the room was dark, he tripped over the wire of something called an intravenous infusion pole, and when the nurse came in a few moments later she found me sleeping soundly but my brother Jason lying on the floor in a daze, blood pouring from above his eye where he'd injured himself.

'Don't let my brother die!' he cried out as the nurse examined his wound.

'Sam's not going to die,' said the nurse. 'Look at him, he's fine. He's fast asleep. You, on the other hand, are going to need stitches. Here, hold this towel to your head and let's go down to my office.'

But my brother Jason was convinced that there was something terribly wrong with me and that, if he left me alone, then something awful would happen. And so he insisted on staying exactly where he was, and eventually the nurse had to sew up his wound right there, and she must have been quite new because she didn't do a very good job.

And *that's* how he got the scar.

I've always loved his injury, because whenever I look at it I think of that story and how he insisted on staying by my side when I was sick. It shows me how much my brother Jason has always loved me. Even when he started growing his hair longer, and I didn't see the scar as often as I used to because he liked to pull his fringe down over his forehead, I knew it was there. And I knew what it meant.

For as long as I can remember, my brother Jason has taken care of me. There were au pairs, of course – *lots* of au pairs – because Mum said if she didn't put her constituents first they'd vote for the other side at the next election and then the country would go to rack and ruin. And Dad said it was important that Mum always won by a substantial margin if she was to continue her climb up the greasy pole.

'It looks good to the party,' he said, 'if she doesn't just win, but wins *big*.'

Most of the au pairs didn't stay very long because they said they were professionals with qualifications, they'd been to university, knew their rights and refused to be treated like slave labour. And Mum always pointed out that, if they were so highly educated, then they'd know that slaves didn't get paid whereas they did, and then she'd turn to Dad and say something like, 'These are the types that go on marches, protesting against everything, but never actually raise a finger to help,' and an argument would break out that took in everything from the failings of the health service to nuclear disarmament, by way of the rising price of Tube tickets and the Middle East peace process.

Sometimes my parents and the au pair would reach some sort of agreement, but it only took a few weeks for things to flare up again, and then the original advertisement would be brought out and the girl (and once a boy) would point out that it said nothing about ironing the parents' clothes, weeding the front garden, or folding thousands of constituency leaflets into envelopes while they were watching television in their own room in their private time. But then Mum would show them the line about 'other general household duties' and everyone would start shouting at each other. The phrase *If you don't like it, you can always leave* came out, and then Mum and Dad would argue, because he'd say it would take an eternity to find another au pair and he'd be stuck at home with 'those bloody children' in the meantime, and Mum would say, *Oh, you just don't want her to go because you like staring at her bum* – this is what *Mum* would say, I'm only *telling* you – and eventually the au pair would announce that she was going on strike for better conditions, and Mum would say, if that was the case, then she could pack her bags and be gone by the following afternoon and good riddance to bad rubbish.

So they came and went like the seasons and I knew not to waste my time growing too close to any of them. And by the time I was ten my brother Jason was already fourteen, and Mum said we didn't need an au pair any more – he could bring me home from school every day unless he had football practice, in which case I was to sit in the stands and do my homework until he was finished. And he said fine, but could he get the same money the au pairs had earned, and Dad said, you live in our house rent-free, you eat our food and make a mess with your football boots and your dirty kit, so how about we call it even?

You might think you know some good footballers but, believe me, you don't know anyone as good as my brother Jason. He started playing football when he was only a toddler, and by the time he was nine years old he'd already had a trial with Arsenal Academy, but they said he wasn't ready yet and wanted to see him again in a year's time. Twelve months later he returned for a follow-up, and the coach said that he'd come on in leaps and bounds in the meantime and there was a place for him there if he wanted it, but to everyone's surprise my brother Jason turned it down. He said that, even though he liked to play at school, he didn't want it to take over his life, and he definitely didn't want to become a professional footballer when he grew up.

'Well, that's just ridiculous,' said Mum, who'd had a huge argument with the head of the Academy the year before when they'd rejected him, and made some vague threats regarding sports funding. 'You've obviously got talent. I've seen you play and you're better than everyone else in your class. You always, you know . . . kick the ball and get it into the net . . . Or sometimes you do anyway.'

'Why not just agree to go for the next seven or eight years?' suggested Dad. 'That's not so long, is it? Just until you finish school, and then you can make a proper decision about your future. It would look very good for Mum if you were signed to a professional football club. The voters would love it.'

'Because I don't want to,' he insisted. 'I just like playing for fun.'

'Fun?' asked Dad, looking at him as if he'd just started speaking a foreign language. 'You're ten years old, Jason! Do you really think your life is supposed to be about fun?'

'I do, actually,' he said.

'Do you know what your problem is, Jason?' asked Mum, who was filing her nails while scanning the newspapers, and he shook his head.

'No,' he said. 'What?'

'You're selfish. You only ever think about yourself.'

And, although I was only six years old at the time and sitting quietly in the corner of the room, I also knew that this was completely untrue, because my brother Jason was the least selfish person I knew.

'Why don't you want to be a famous footballer?' I asked him once when I was lying on his bed and he was playing CDs for me and telling me why each song he played was the greatest song ever written and how I needed to broaden my musical knowledge and stop listening to rubbish. As I looked around the room, I saw pictures of footballers on the walls, but then again there was also a poster of Australia and another of Shrek, and I didn't think he wanted to be a continent or a cartoon ogre either.

'I just don't,' he said with a shrug. 'Just because I'm good at something, Sam, doesn't mean I want to spend the rest of my life doing it. There are lots of other things I might want to do instead.'

And, to be honest, that sounded pretty reasonable to me.

Last year, when I was thirteen, my English teacher gave our class an essay to write over the weekend called 'The Person I Most Admire'. Seven girls wrote about Kate Middleton, five boys wrote about David Beckham and there were three more on Iron Man. After that it was a mixture of people like the Queen, Jacqueline Wilson and Barack Obama. My nemesis, David Fugue, who has bullied me relentlessly since the day I tried to welcome him to our street, wrote about Kim Jong-un, the Supreme Leader of North Korea, and, when our teacher, Mr Lowry, gave him eighty-seven different reasons why Kim Jong-un was not a positive role model, David Fugue waited until he'd finished before saying that he needed to be very careful what he said or he might find himself in serious trouble. He claimed that he played online every night with Kim Jong-un and that they'd become great friends. Just a word from him, he said, and Mr Lowry might find himself on the wrong side of an unpleasant accident when he was walking home one evening. That didn't go down very well, and David got a letter home to his parents and had to stand up in front of the entire class the next day and

apologize for making a casual reference to violence at
school.

I was the only person who didn't write about a famous
person. I wrote about my brother Jason.

FIVE THINGS I WROTE ABOUT IN MY ESSAY

1. How he'd got the scar on his forehead when I
   was just a baby, although I lied and said I still
   had a hole in my heart and could die any day
   without warning, which isn't true as the doctors
   fixed it, but it won me a lot of sympathy anyway.
2. How he'd once saved me from being run over by
   pushing me out of the way just in time, and when
   the driver pulled over to tell me off – even though
   he had *clearly* been at fault because it was a zebra
   crossing – my brother Jason chased him back to
   his car, looking like he was going to kill him if he
   caught up with him.
3. How he was captain of the football team and
   could have been a professional footballer if he'd
   wanted to, but there were lots of other things he
   wanted to do instead.
4. How he was going out with Penny Wilson, who
   everyone knew was the best-looking girl in
   school.

5. How he'd saved me from being eaten alive by Brutus, a horrible dog who lives down the road from us and who always starts slobbering when he sees me, as if he thinks I might be the most delicious treat on the planet.

FIVE THINGS I DIDN'T WRITE ABOUT IN MY ESSAY

1. How, only a few weeks earlier, he'd had a big argument with Mum and Dad, telling them it was ridiculous that they were never at home, that they always put Mum's job ahead of us and that he couldn't be expected to take care of me forever when he had his own life to live. What would happen when he went to university? he asked. But Mum had said that by then I'd be old enough to look after myself, and he'd just thrown his hands in the air and said, *I give up*, and taken to his room and refused to speak to anyone, even me, for a full day afterwards.

2. How he wasn't on Facebook, Twitter, Instagram or Snapchat because he said he couldn't stand everyone always going around with their heads in their phones, doing things only so that they could photograph them but never actually experiencing them.

3. How I'd caught him and Penny Wilson kissing in his bedroom the previous week when I ran in without knocking, and he'd chased me out with a tennis racket.

4. How he said that when he was eighteen he was going to vote for the other side and not Mum's lot, because every one of them was corrupt and they were only in it for themselves.

5. How he'd been growing his blond hair long for a few months now, and putting all these stupid layers in it, even though everyone, including me, thought it made him look a bit girly.

Some of my friends seemed a bit embarrassed for me, writing about my brother like that, but he *was* the person I most admired, so it seemed only right that he should be the subject of my essay. Whenever I needed him, he was there. When I was a child and had a bad dream, he'd always let me crawl into bed with him and would tell me that everything was all right. When I started to struggle with reading and Dad said they needed to have me tested and it turned out that I had a reading problem, it was my brother Jason who sat down with me every night and helped me with my homework, and, no matter how frustrated I got when the words and the letters started to dance around the page in a way that didn't make sense, he never ever got impatient with me – he never shouted, *Just read what's on the bloody page!* the way Dad did – and he always told me that it would be fine in time, that he'd help me, that he'd always be there for me, that we were brothers, and nothing could ever come between us.

I believed him too.

I knew something was wrong with my brother Jason for about a year and a half before he told us his secret. Although he was still my best friend, he'd started to grow a little more distant towards me – towards *all* of us – and sometimes he would shut himself in his room and refuse to open the door for hours at a time. I hated when he did that because he'd never excluded me from anything in the past, and it didn't matter how often I knocked, he'd just shout at me to go away and leave him alone.

Once, when I got home from school, I found him crying on his bed and I didn't know what to do because it felt like such a reversal of our roles. I was the one who was sometimes sad, especially when I got teased about my reading, and he was always the one who helped to cheer me up. It wasn't that I didn't want to be there for him too, it was just that I didn't know how to be a big brother when I'd always been the little brother. It frightened me to see him like that. I asked him what was wrong, and when he sat up I could see from his face that he'd been crying for ages, because his cheeks were red and his eyes were all puffy.

'Nothing's wrong,' he said.

'Of course it is. You've been crying.'

'Just go to your room, Sam. Please. I don't want to talk about it.'

And, because I didn't know what to say or how to help him, that's what I did.

'Teenagers,' Dad said when I asked him about this. 'That's the worst of having children, you know. They all turn into teenagers. If they could just go from twelve to twenty overnight, everything would be a lot easier.'

'But what's he doing in there?' I asked.

'I dread to think. Some things are best left alone, if you ask me.'

'Don't you think he seems different in some way?'

'In what way?'

'I don't know. Quieter. Angrier. Upset, a lot of the time.'

'The only thing that's different about him, as far as I can see, is that hair of his. I've asked him to cut it off, but he refuses. I don't think he realizes how ridiculous he looks with it hanging down over his shoulders like that. It's like he thinks it's the 1970s and he's the blonde girl out of ABBA.' He paused for a moment and smiled to himself, as if he was having some sort of weird flashback. Then he sighed and looked all dreamy-eyed.

'Dad!' I said, to snap him out of it.

'Sorry,' he said. 'It's just . . . Agnetha and I had a very special relationship when I was your age. But, honestly, sometimes I feel like just waiting until your brother's asleep and going in there with a pair of scissors and cutting it myself.'

'Something's not right,' I said. 'He's sort of . . .'

'Sort of what?' asked Dad, turning to me, and for a moment I thought I could see a look of concern on his face, something I hadn't seen very often in the past.

'All I know is that he's not the same old Jason,' I said. 'There's something on his mind. Something important. I can tell.'

'Oh, for heaven's sake, Sam,' said Dad, turning back to his computer, where a spreadsheet lay open with the names of everyone from the parliamentary party listed, some with green ticks beside their names, some with red crosses and some with yellow question marks. 'We've all got things on our minds. You should try figuring out who this lot will get behind when the moment comes. I wouldn't worry about it if I was you.'

'But I *am* worried about it!' I protested.

He stared at me and his eyes held mine for a moment longer than was necessary.

'You *have* noticed something, haven't you?' I said.

'No,' he said.

'You *have*!' I insisted. 'I can see it on your face.'

'I haven't,' he shouted. 'Now stop bothering me, all right? I have work to do.'

'You *have*,' I muttered as I walked away.

But nothing concerned me as much as what happened on the day that I came to think of as the Very Strange Afternoon. I'd come home from school earlier than usual – I was supposed to have swimming practice but a seven-year-old had peed in the pool earlier so that was the end of that – and when I put my key in the front door and turned the lock I heard my brother Jason calling out from the kitchen.

'Who's that?' he roared, and something in his tone made me freeze on the spot. I had never heard him sound so anxious before.

'It's only me,' I said, throwing my bag on the floor and making my way down the corridor to see what was in the fridge.

'Stay where you are!' he shouted, and I stopped with one foot literally about to make contact with the floor, like a cartoon character.

'What's going on?' I asked.

'Nothing. Just stay exactly where you are, all right? No, go downstairs to Mum's office!'

I took a step backwards in confusion and glanced at the door that led to the basement, where I'm not supposed to go. *Ever*. Mum says that it's a violation of her sacred space. And that she keeps state secrets down there too. I asked her once whether she had the nuclear codes in her office, and she just laughed and shook her head, saying, *Not yet, Sam. Not yet*.

'But I'm hungry,' I said. 'I just want a sandwich, that's all,' I added, but then he shouted again, and this time I heard such a mixture of anger and terror in his voice that a chill ran through me.

'Sam,' he shouted. 'I'm telling you to go downstairs to Mum's office *right now*, do you hear me? You are *not* to set foot in the living room or the kitchen. Go downstairs and stay there until I come to get you. Or I'll never speak to you again. EVER. For the rest of your life. Do you understand?'

I could feel myself growing pale. My brother Jason had never spoken to me like that before, and he'd certainly never threatened to stop speaking to me. I was frightened and confused all at the same time. I wondered whether there were burglars in the house and he was being held at gunpoint and that's why he didn't want me to go in. I thought about phoning the police.

'Please, Sam,' he said a moment later, his voice quieter now, and I could tell that he was close to tears. 'Please, just do as I ask. Please. I'll come downstairs and get you in a few minutes. I promise.'

And so I went downstairs to Mum's office and sat there, afraid to touch anything in case she found out, and waited for almost twenty minutes before I heard the door open upstairs and my brother Jason's voice calling to tell me that I could come back up again.

'Sorry about that,' he said, unable to look me in the eye, even though I was staring at him in complete confusion because he was acting as if nothing unusual had just taken place. 'I was finishing some really difficult homework, that's all, and I didn't want to be disturbed.'

I said nothing. I knew that he was lying but didn't want to challenge him. The whole thing had seemed so bizarre. But then I realized what it must have been. He must have had a girl in there, and maybe it wasn't Penny Wilson but someone else and he didn't want me to know in case I told someone. Because there seemed to be a faint trace of lipstick on his lips and I could smell perfume in the air.

Mum and Dad were both home the night he told us his secret, which was unusual enough in itself. It was the summer holidays and they were in the living room, Mum reading through some position papers while Dad kept muttering names and saying that he or she was another one they'd have to get on side if Mum was ever to reach what he called the Top Job. I was doing my best to read a Sherlock Holmes story, putting my fingers under the words and using my pencil to separate sentences and phrases just like I'd been shown. I struggled so much with reading because of my dyslexia, but I still wanted books all the time and didn't care if it took me ages to finish them. I was in the middle of 'The Man with the Twisted Lip' when my brother Jason came into the living room and said that he had something he wanted to talk to us about.

'Can it wait?' asked Mum. 'I'm just trying to –'

'If you need money, get a summer job,' said Dad. 'We're not the Bank of –'

'It can't wait and I don't need money,' he said, and something in his tone made us all stop what we were doing and turn to look at him. He sat down in the middle of the sofa, as far away from all of us as possible, and started to speak.

'This isn't easy,' he said.

'What isn't easy?' asked Mum.

'What I'm about to tell you.'

'Well, spit it out, Jason,' said Dad. 'We don't have all night.'

He swallowed, and I could see that he was trembling a little. He put one hand in the other before him as if to keep himself steady, but his voice still shook when he spoke.

He told us that he'd known something for a long time, something about himself that was very difficult to come to terms with. He told us that he'd always felt it, ever since he was a small child, and that he'd convinced himself it was something he would just have to live with because everyone would hate him if they knew the truth. But recently he'd started to think that perhaps he didn't have to lie, that maybe he could tell people, be *honest* with them, and maybe, just maybe, they'd understand.

'You're going to say you're gay, aren't you?' asked Mum, putting a hand to her mouth, but my brother Jason shook his head.

'No, it's not that,' he said.

21

'Jake Tomlin is gay,' I said, but no one was listening to me as usual. Jake Tomlin was a boy in my year who'd already told everyone he was gay, but no one was mean to him because he was very strong, and it was obvious that he'd bash anyone who even tried to make a joke about it. I quite liked Jake, but we weren't too friendly because he was more into sport than me.

'Can you just hear me out?' asked my brother Jason.

'Is that Penny girl pregnant?' asked Mum.

'You're not sick, are you?' I asked, suddenly frightened. 'You're not dying?'

'No,' he said. 'It's nothing like that. I'm fine.'

'Do you promise?' I asked.

'I promise,' he said. 'I'm not sick, I'm not gay and Penny's not pregnant.'

'Good,' I said, and I felt myself growing upset at the idea of him having anything wrong with him. 'Because you're the best brother in the world, you know that.' I could hear how sentimental that sounded but I didn't care. Right at that moment I just needed to say those words out loud and him to hear them.

There was a long silence then while he just stared at the floor, but finally he looked up again and shook his head. 'But that's just it, Sam,' he said. 'I don't think I'm your brother at all. In fact, I'm pretty sure I'm not.'

'Not his brother?' asked Mum. 'What on earth are you talking about? Of course you're his brother. I gave birth to both of you, so I think I would know.'

I stared at him in confusion. 'What do you mean?' I asked.

'Exactly what I say,' he replied. 'I don't think I'm your brother. I think I'm actually your sister.'

2

Bad Neighbours

I first met my nemesis, David Fugue, when we were both seven years old. Mrs Henderson, who had lived in the house two doors down from us for about three hundred years, died, and her granddaughter immediately put the property up for sale. I'd always liked Mrs Henderson, who used to take her false teeth out to show me how easily they popped back in again, and she even let me take her fake eye into school once for Show and Tell, which made two of my classmates – *both of them boys!* – throw up. She'd lost her eye in the war, she said, but couldn't remember how. Which always seemed a bit odd to me. If I lost my eye, I was pretty sure I'd remember what happened to it.

Anyway, the business of who was going to buy Mrs

Henderson's house became something of an obsession with Mum and Dad, who took turns pretending to adjust the curtains in the front room or going outside to inspect the garden whenever a strange car pulled up on the street. There were a lot of mutterings about house prices going down and not wanting the neighbourhood to turn into something it was never intended to be.

'This a very settled area, Sam,' Mum explained to me when I asked her why it mattered who lived two doors down from us when we wouldn't even be able to hear them if they had parties or played loud music. We couldn't even hear what was going on in the house next to ours as the walls were so thick. 'It's what you might call a *local* area.'

'Aren't all areas local areas?' I asked, and she shook her head and looked at me as if I hadn't an ounce of sense.

'Everyone gets along here,' she said. 'And it would be a shame if that were to change. Mrs Henderson was wonderful, of course, and she'll be missed. To be honest, it would have been better if she'd just gone on and on forever, making sarcastic comments and frightening the door-to-door salesmen. I always thought of her as a sort of Maggie Smith character.'

'Who's Maggie Smith?' I asked.

'Professor McGonagall,' she told me. 'From the Harry Potter movies.'

'Oh yes,' I replied, not knowing that Maggie Smith had false teeth and a fake eye. She'd kept that well hidden in the films.

'And I'd hate to see her legacy tarnished in some way,' continued Mum while I frowned, not sure what she was talking about. 'She wouldn't have wanted just *anyone* living in her house, don't you think? But what can you do? The country isn't like it was when I was a girl. Now don't get me wrong, Sam, I want to see this part of London open to everyone –'

'We both do,' piped up Dad, who was sitting at the kitchen table going through Mum's diary for the following week.

'Live and let live, that's my motto. Always has been. But for a community to flourish, everyone has to be part of that community. We have to help each other out, to act in a neighbourly fashion, to feel comfortable living side by side.'

'You know what she's saying, don't you?' asked my brother Jason, who had been sitting in an armchair flicking through Mum's copy of *Vogue*, probably because there were always pictures of girls in their underwear in there. (Trust me on that. Mum threw them in the recycle bin when she was finished with them, but I always fished them out and kept them in my special box with the lock and key at the back of my wardrobe.) 'No blacks, no Pakis, no Irish.'

A silence descended on the room, and I watched as Mum slowly turned away from the window, her face growing pale.

'What did you just say?' she asked quietly.

'You heard me,' replied my brother Jason, although he didn't sound quite as confident now and I could hear a certain tremor in his voice. Dad had closed his laptop and was staring at him with a look of astonishment on his face.

'Was that supposed to be a joke?' asked Mum.

'Oh, come on,' he said, slamming the magazine down on the table. 'It's all middle-class values around here, isn't it? Keep like with like. Don't let the foreigners in. You don't even have any black friends, do you?'

'That's not true,' said Dad. 'Stephen and Angie were round here for dinner two weeks ago, remember?'

'Well, besides them,' said my brother Jason. I was surprised he'd forgotten Stephen and Angie as they'd known Mum and Dad forever and Stephen was his godfather.

'And how often do we go out for drinks with Jack and Roger?'

'Jack and Roger aren't black,' said my brother Jason. 'They're gay.'

'Yes, but if you're accusing us of some sort of prejudice, I'm just pointing out that you're wrong. And, actually, it's an appalling thing to suggest.'

'I agree,' said Mum, and I felt like leaving the room because even I was a bit disappointed in my brother Jason, and it wasn't something that happened often. 'In fact, I can't even believe that you would say such a thing. If that's what you think of us, then clearly you don't know us at all.'

'All right, I'm sorry,' he said eventually. 'I was wrong.'

'Yes. You were.'

'But you can't blame me for thinking that you're not entirely interested in the lives of minorities. After all –'

'You know, there's a car pulling up in front of the house right now,' I said, looking out of the window as a couple emerged with a son around my age and a daughter a year or so older, each one seeming a little less impressed by what they saw than the other.

'Let's have a look,' said Mum, pushing me out of the way, and I practically fell off the sofa she was so keen to see who they might be. 'Now!' she cried, turning round in triumph, a broad smile on her face. 'He's black, she's white and their children are a bit of both. And do you know what I'm going to do, Jason? I'm going to go over there right now and tell them what a wonderful neighbourhood this is. Sam, hand me some of those election leaflets. It won't do any harm to secure their vote from the start.'

In the end, the couple who had been looking at Mrs Henderson's house – the Fugues – bought it, and the day they moved in, while Mum was on the internet trying to find a politically correct present to give them as a welcome gift, I made the mistake of trying to befriend their son.

'I thought I'd come over and say hello,' I told him, having made my way down the street while he was standing outside his front gate, looking around with an expression on his face that suggested the sewers had overflowed and ruined his new espadrilles. 'You've just arrived, haven't you?' I was actually quite glad to see him because there weren't any other boys my age on Rutherford Road and I'd never really made any close friends at school. No one ever came over to stay the night or invited me on holiday to the South of France. I wasn't quite sure where I'd gone wrong on this, but somehow it had just never happened for me. I think it had something to do with the fact that I was so bad at reading. It made me seem invisible a lot of the time.

Not that being invisible was always a bad thing. After all, it meant that I didn't get asked questions by teachers too often, which I was glad about because I hated it when everyone looked at me if I didn't realize that the word *solitary* in a book was the word *solitary*. Or the word *coincidental* was the word *coincidental*. Although it wasn't just big words that confused me. Sometimes, words with lots of vowels were difficult too. Like *iguana*. Or *evacuee*. Although, that said, words with no vowels at all – like *rhythm* – could be troublesome too. There was no real logic to any of it.

'Yes, but it's only a temporary thing,' said David, looking me up and down as if I was a winter coat he was considering returning. 'We're downsizing for a year or two, that's all. The recession, you know. It hit us quite hard. Our real house is a mansion with a heated swimming pool and a cinema room in the basement. We'll only be here until the economy picks up again.'

I stared at him, never having heard anyone my age speaking in such elevated terms before. I didn't care about the economy and I didn't know much about how other people lived, but from what I saw on television I could tell that our home was a lot better than the homes of many people in England. All the houses on our street were red brick, with a good-sized garden out the back, and each one had four floors. Oxford Street wasn't far away. And someone who Mum and Dad referred to as 'a minor royal who couldn't get a grace-and-favour flat at Kensington Palace' lived at the end of the road in number one with her collection of antique mirrors and a butler with a beard.

'Right,' I said. 'What's your name anyway?'

'David Fugue,' he told me. 'You're probably familiar with my family. We have a chair at Magdalen College. I bet you can't spell Magdalen College. Go on, try. I'll give you five pounds if you get it right.'

'I'm Sam Waver,' I said. 'I live a couple of doors down at number ten.'

'Waver?' he replied, frowning. 'Nothing to do with Deborah Waver, I suppose?'

'She's my mother,' I said.

'Oh, Lord,' he said, shaking his head. 'That's all we need. A politician on the street. What next? A film star? An American? You know she's completely corrupt, of course,' he added, leaning forward and lowering his voice. 'She's only in the Cabinet because she's got some dirt on the PM. And she takes backhanders.'

I didn't know what any of this meant but didn't much like the sound of it. I wondered what my brother Jason would do at such a moment, but since I knew that he didn't like it when people said nasty things about other people, I decided to stick up for her.

'My mother is climbing her way to the top of the greasy pole *actually*,' I told him, standing up straight and feeling proud that I could repeat the words I'd heard Dad say on so many occasions in the past. 'They say she might get the top job in the end. So you should be careful what you say, because one day she'll have the nuclear codes.'

'My father could probably have been PM,' said David. 'But he'd never have wanted a job like that. He's far too intelligent for it. And you know true power resides mostly behind the scenes, don't you? The PM's just a puppet of the global multinationals, nothing more.'

'Yes,' I said, though in fact I neither knew it nor even understood what he was talking about.

'Anyway, there'll be an election soon, I expect,' he continued. 'And something tells me your mother will be out on her ear then.'

'You're not very friendly, are you?' I said, scrunching up my face angrily. 'I only came over to say hello.'

'Yes, well, I'm not really in the market for new friends, if that's what you're hoping for,' he replied. 'I've got lots back at home at my real house, you see.'

'The one you lost, you mean?'

'We haven't lost it,' he snapped. 'This is just a temporary *snafu*, that's all.'

'What's a *snafu*?' I asked.

'A blip.'

'What's a blip?'

'I'm sorry, is English your first language?' he asked.

'*Oui, bien sûr*,' I said, proud of my little joke, but he simply rolled his eyes.

'Oh, Lord,' he said. 'What have we let ourselves in for?'

'Maybe my mum was right,' I said, growing angry now. 'We should keep this place local.'

He raised an eyebrow and produced a tiny notebook from his back pocket and a miniature-sized pen. 'Your mum said that, did she?' he asked, scribbling the phrase down. 'And what exactly was she getting at?'

'Nothing,' I said, sensing that I might have just said something wrong. 'She's not racist, if that's what you mean. My brother Jason said she was but then Dad pointed out that they couldn't be because they're friends with Stephen and Angie and –'

'And I assume these people are black?'

'Yes,' I said. 'And Jack and Roger are gay.'

'Who are Jack and Roger?'

'Friends of my parents.'

'So they have two black friends and two gay friends. How modern! They must be very pleased with themselves!'

'Oh, shut up,' I said. 'I've never met anyone as stupid as you in my entire life.'

'Typical prole,' he replied.

'I said shut up.'

'You shut up, prole. Know your place!'

'You've only just got here! I was here first!'

'And we won't be staying. Once the economy –'

'Yeah, yeah, yeah,' I said, turning away and marching back home, seething inwardly. Who was this boy to arrive in our neighbourhood and start talking to me like this and calling me names? I hated him already.

As things turned out, that was probably the friendliest conversation we ever had for, although we never engaged in a physical fight over the years that followed, he needled away at me, pretending that he was better than all of us and constantly claiming that once the economy was fixed, which it never seemed to be, he and his family would be leaving forever and returning to their real house, the mansion with the heated swimming pool and the cinema room in the basement.

EIGHT THINGS I WANTED TO HAPPEN TO MY
NEMESIS, DAVID FUGUE

1. Be eaten by a shark.
2. Be kept in a basement by a madman and given nothing to eat but green vegetables for breakfast, lunch and dinner.
3. Be forced to listen to Ed Sheeran albums played on a continuous loop for a week.
4. Be adopted by a family who live in New Zealand.
5. Call our maths teacher, Miss Whiteside, 'Mum' one day in class, because no one *ever* lives that down.
6. Be found kissing himself in the mirror in the boys' toilets and for someone to take a photograph of it and send it to everyone.
7. Be sent to a Young Offender Institution.
8. Wake up one morning with about twenty spots all over his face.

But although David Fugue and I despised each other, I never imagined that he would learn my brother Jason's secret and be the first to reveal it to the world. On the day that happened, it felt as if he'd been waiting a long time for his triumph and was determined to savour every moment.

*

The morning after my brother Jason told us his secret, we were all sitting around the breakfast table, barely looking at each other.

'I think it's best if we try to pretend last night never took place,' said Mum eventually, when all that could be heard was the scraping of butter on toast and the slurping of hot cups of tea. 'It was just one of those strange evenings that happen from time to time and are best forgotten about, like the night your father sang karaoke in front of the Queen.'

Dad frowned. He liked to think he was a good singer, but he really wasn't.

'If I recall correctly,' he said, 'she applauded at the end.'

'That's because she was being polite. Her Majesty is *always* polite. Even when someone is butchering "A Crazy Little Thing Called Love".'

Mum glanced over at Bradley, the ministerial driver, who came in for a coffee most mornings while she was getting ready to leave the house, and asked him to wait outside in the car. 'The best thing that can happen right now,' she continued when he was gone, 'is that we all just move on and act like it was some sort of strange dream. Jason, you're a teenage boy and you're confused, that's all it is. You'll grow out of it, I promise you. You just have to give it time. There's been all this talk about

37

people being transgender on the radio and on television –'
and when she said the word *transgender* she used her
fingers to make inverted comma signs in the air – 'and
really you're just trying to be different, to forge your
own identity. Teenagers always do that. Why, when I
was your age I said I wanted to be a private detective
simply because I'd read too many Nancy Drew books.
And remember last summer, when your brother couldn't
stop listening to Ed Sheeran records?'

'It's true,' I said, nodding. 'And now I look back and
wonder, what on earth was I thinking?'

'So I don't want to hear you ever repeat the things
you told us to anyone,' she continued. 'All right?'

My brother Jason looked up, and when I saw his
expression, lost and lonely, I turned away.

'Your mother and I stayed up late last night talking it
over,' said Dad, reaching across and placing a hand on
my brother Jason's shoulder and patting him as if he
was a puppy. 'It's obvious that you're going through
some sort of personal crisis, but we're your parents, we
love you and we're going to get you help.'

'What kind of help?' he asked, looking up hopefully.
Perhaps he too thought that there was some way out of
this for him.

'Medical help,' said Mum.

'What kind of medical help?'

'Well, I don't know, do I?' she replied in frustration. 'I'm not a doctor. Pills, perhaps. Or hypnosis. Electroshock therapy.'

'What's that?' he asked.

'I'm not entirely sure but I think it involves strapping lots of wires to you, and whenever you think something – something you shouldn't think – then you get a shock. A fairly light one, I mean. Not enough to cause any permanent damage. And eventually you become too terrified to think it any more.'

'What?' he asked, sounding petrified.

'Actually,' said Dad, 'I was wondering earlier whether it might be a good idea to ask Hector's advice.'

'Hector who?' asked Mum.

'The Health Secretary, Hector Dunaway, of course. How many Hectors do you know? He must have a list of the top people in the field.'

Mum stared at him for a moment before sitting back in her chair, folding her arms and laughing as she shook her head. 'I'm sorry, Alan, but have you completely lost your mind?' she asked. 'You want me to tell Hector that our son thinks he's a girl?'

'The word is transgender,' said my brother Jason.

'I know the word,' said Mum, glaring at him. 'I used

it only a few moments ago. I'm just trying not to make us too comfortable with it, that's all,'

'Why not?' I asked.

'Because,' she said.

'Great answer,' said my brother Jason.

'The point is that talking to Hector would be a massive mistake. For all we know, he might have his own leadership ambitions.'

'Good point,' said Dad, looking down at the table, suitably chastised. 'Terrible idea. Don't tell Hector.'

'Honestly, I can't believe you even suggested it.'

'I said it was a terrible idea,' said Dad irritably.

'Karaoke was a terrible idea,' she said. 'Telling Hector was just insane!'

'All right! Let's move on!'

'We tell *no one*,' said Mum, turning to look at each of us in turn. 'Absolutely no one. We treat this as if Jason has murdered someone.'

'But I haven't murdered anyone,' he said.

'No, of course not. Perhaps that came out wrong. But remember, if you actually *did* murder someone, then we, as your parents, would do everything we could to protect you.'

'Are you actually saying,' he asked, raising his voice now in frustration, 'that if I came home one day and told you that I'd just murdered someone, you'd cover it up? Or that you think being transgender is just as bad as being a murderer?'

'Oh, for God's sake, I don't know what I'm saying,' roared Mum, banging both hands down on the table before her so all the plates, cups and glasses shook a little while the rest of us jumped in surprise. 'And, no, of course I'm not saying that. I'm just ... I'm just trying to make sense of all this and do what's best for everyone, OK? This is all new to me – can't you understand that? You can't expect us to have answers for everything immediately. You have to be fair to us too, you know. You've been thinking about this for a long time. It's all new to your dad and me!'

My brother Jason said nothing, but I could see from his face that he was probably regretting having told us anything at all. He hadn't eaten any breakfast either. Even his glass of orange juice remained completely untouched, and most days he got through so much orange juice that Dad said he was going to turn into a tangerine.

'And you, Sam,' said Mum, pointing a finger at me. 'You're not to breathe a word about any of this to anyone, understand? I know what a little blabbermouth you can be.'

I nodded. She didn't need to worry. I had absolutely no intention whatsoever of talking about it. The last thing I needed was any more trouble at school.

'And as for you . . .' said Mum, turning to my brother Jason, who, to my shock, put his head in his hands and started to cry.

'Why are you crying?' asked Dad, reaching over and placing a hand on his elbow. 'Can't you see that we're trying to help you?'

'I'm sorry,' he said.

'Sorry for what? For crying or for making that speech last night?'

'For everything,' he said.

'I still don't understand,' I said. 'Why do you think you're a girl? You have a willy. I know you do. I've seen it.'

'Sam!' shouted Mum. 'No willies at the breakfast table!'

'Sorry,' I said. 'But he does.'

'Your mother simply means that we'd prefer not to talk about willies at this time of the morning,' said Dad.

'Oh, OK,' I said. 'So when can we talk about them?'

'We can't,' said Mum.

'Why not?'

'Because they're disgusting.'

42

'Ah,' said Dad quietly. 'Actually that explains a lot.'

'There's nothing disgusting about willies,' said my brother Jason. 'Don't tell him that. It'll warp him.'

'Says the boy who wants to pretend that he doesn't have one!' shouted Mum.

'I'm not pretending I don't have one! I know I have one. I just feel that –'

'We're doing it again,' cried Mum, shouting louder now than I'd ever heard her shout before. 'We're *still* talking about willies. Despite me making it absolutely clear that I don't want to discuss them! Honestly, if I hear another word from any of you about –'

There was a tap on the kitchen door and Bradley poked his head in. 'Sorry to interrupt, Secretary of State,' he said. 'Only if we're going to make the Cabinet meeting we should probably leave fairly sharpish. You know what the traffic is like at this time of the morning.'

'Yes, all right,' said Mum with a sigh as she stood up. 'Look, we'll talk about this again when I get home,' she added, gathering up her red boxes as she walked towards the door. 'And when I say we'll talk about this again when I get home, what I actually mean is that we'll never talk about it again for the rest of our lives, understand?'

Which, like so many things that had happened over the previous twenty-four hours, made absolutely no sense to me whatsoever.

Maybe it was because no one in the family wanted to talk to my brother Jason about what he was going through that he chose to confide in someone else. A few weeks passed and we were all behaving as if nothing had ever happened. If I walked into a room and tried to speak to either Mum or Dad, they said they were too busy to talk, and although I was desperate to know what they were thinking, I was frightened of introducing the subject because I, like them, didn't want to believe that it could possibly be true. To talk about it was to make it seem more real and I don't think any of us were ready for that.

My brother Jason, of course, had become even quieter than before and was now spending most of his time alone in his room, but perhaps we should have guessed that he would talk to his girlfriend, Penny Wilson, who was without doubt the most beautiful girl I'd ever seen. She looked like one of the girls in Mum's *Vogue*s, particularly the girl on page 126 of the June 2017 issue, which was my favourite issue of all time and always seemed to be at the top of my special box with the lock and key at the back of my wardrobe. Although, as pretty as she was, she wasn't always very nice.

Penny and my brother Jason had only been dating for a few months, but since then she'd spent quite a bit of time at our house. At first I hated it when she called round, partly because she kept the two of us apart, but mostly because I felt embarrassed when I was around her. My first introduction to her had been on the afternoon I discovered them kissing on his bed, and my most dominant memory of that moment wasn't how he had chased me out with a tennis racket but how her blouse had been unbuttoned as she lay there, the pink bra that she was wearing underneath, and the pale, smooth skin of her stomach. That image had been tattooed on to my memory ever since, confusing, exciting and frightening me in equal parts. I wanted to put my hand on her skin too, and lie on a bed with her just as my brother Jason had done. For weeks afterwards I thought about her, and then I started to dream about her, and the worst of it all was she continued to treat me like a child, ruffling my hair whenever she saw me and telling me that I was going to be a heartbreaker when I was 'all grown up'.

But Penny was the next person my brother Jason told, and even though I'm sure that she was as shocked as we were, she promised not to tell a soul. A few days later, however, she sent him a text telling him that she was no longer his girlfriend and was now going out with Jack Savonarola, the half-Italian goalkeeper on the football team who all the girls said had dreamy eyes, but that she'd always be there for him if he needed a friend.

This was just one more thing for him to be upset about, but still, no matter how much I wanted to, I couldn't find a way to talk to him about it.

School started again and things began to settle down into the usual boring routine. But just when I was thinking that my brother Jason's secret was safe, my nemesis, David Fugue, sprang his surprise.

Everyone knew that Mr Lowry was fixated on the Tudors. No matter what we were discussing, somehow he always managed to bring every conversation back to them. It was an obsession.

'The thing is, it's one of the most interesting periods in the history of the British Isles,' he told us on the day his dreams were finally realized and we arrived at the part of the curriculum where we were going to study them. 'So much drama, so much intrigue. And despite the fact that there were only five Tudor monarchs their legend has endured throughout the centuries. We've only had six female sovereigns on these islands and two of them were Tudors. And what characters each monarch was! The bellicose nature of Henry the Seventh, claiming the throne from the Welsh mountains and seeing the usurper Richard the Third off at the Battle of Bosworth Field. And then the extraordinary story of his son, Henry the Eighth, and his six wives, a prince who started off with such good ambitions but who turned out to be a tyrant. The three children who succeeded him, the only monarch ever to sire three different sovereigns. And, as you may know, the Tudors lie at the heart of almost every novel written by an English novelist over the last ten years. It's a simply endless cavalcade of fiction! But, for me, the most fascinating of them all is Queen Elizabeth the First. Do you know why?'

We all stared at him in silence. We had no idea. And, if we were honest, we didn't really care.

'Because she changed the view that the world had of women,' he told us. 'She proved that a woman could not only rule but rule effectively. While her father had spent most of his reign obsessed with the idea of leaving a son on the throne of England, Elizabeth didn't care about any of that. She lived in the present. What happened after she was gone didn't matter to her in the slightest.'

'Didn't she want a husband?' asked someone from the back of the room.

'And leave herself vulnerable to being ruled by a man?' asked Mr Lowry. 'No! And, believe me, in those days that's exactly what would have happened. Her husband would have assumed the throne and she would have been condemned to a minor place in history. No, Elizabeth decided that she would never marry. She saw herself as neither king nor queen but simply as sovereign. Neither man nor woman. Completely without gender.'

'A bit like Jason Waver,' said David Fugue out of the blue, and I looked up, not entirely sure that I'd heard him right.

'What was that, David?' asked Mr Lowry, looking at him with a baffled expression on his face.

'I said, she sounds a bit like Jason Waver, sir. Sam's brother. *Neither man nor woman. Completely without gender.*'

The entire class turned to look at me in confusion, and I felt my heart start to beat faster inside my chest as my face grew red. My invisibility was starting to fade.

'I have absolutely no idea what you're talking about,' said Mr Lowry, shaking his head. 'I'm talking about Queen Elizabeth the First and you're talking about –'

'Oh, haven't you heard, sir?' asked David, grinning

like the cat who'd got the cream. 'It turns out that Sam's brother has decided that he wants to be a girl.'

Everyone was turning to each other now, mouths open in amazement. Not entirely certain what was happening but sure that there must be some reason for it. A great scandal about to unfold.

'He wants to be a girl?' asked Mr Lowry, turning to look at me. 'I'm sorry, I don't quite know what's –'

'Oh, sir!' cried David, rolling his eyes and raising his voice now. 'Isn't it obvious? Sam's brother is a *tranny*. He told Penny Wilson that he's not a boy at all, that he thinks he's a girl trapped inside a boy's body. He's a total *freak*.'

'That's rubbish,' said Adam Connors, who sat behind me. 'Sam's brother is the best footballer in the school!'

'So?' asked David. 'What has that got to do with anything? You think that means he can't be a tranny?'

'Yes,' said Adam, who everyone knew was the best footballer in our year. Any slight on my brother Jason was a slight on him.

'All right, that's enough,' said Mr Lowry, raising his voice – a rare thing in itself – and slapping the eraser from the whiteboard on the desk to restore order.

The conversation in the class immediately stopped and I could tell that David Fugue was grinning at me,

49

delighted by the trouble he'd started. Turning away, I glanced around the room and I could see that every set of eyes was upon me, waiting for me to say something. But what could I say? They knew. Everyone knew. Stumbling out of my seat, I almost tripped over my bag as I charged out of the room, leaving the sound of laughter behind me, racing towards the boys' toilets, where I flung myself inside a cubicle, locking the door just in time before I threw up the entire contents of my breakfast into the bowl.

Right at that moment I was convinced that my life was over. And I blamed my brother Jason for it.

3

By the Lakes

When half-term arrived and we had a week off school, it came as something of a relief to me not to have to deal with all the gossip any more, and I can only imagine what a release it was for my brother Jason, who was keeping his head down and spending more time in his room than with his friends. Rumours had been swirling around the school like plastic bags blowing in the wind, and almost no one was speaking to me, but whenever I walked into a room I could hear people sniggering behind my back. Someone put a bra in my locker, and when I took it out, intending to throw it in the bin, one of the janitors happened to be walking by and he told me that I was a filthy good-for-nothing, perving over girls' clothes, and I needed locking up.

'Steal it off someone's washing line, did you?' he asked, practically spitting in my face. 'Wouldn't have been tolerated in my day. Bring back National Service, that's what I say.'

Someone else left a make-up case on my desk, and when I picked it up the powder flew out, falling all over my jumper, and everyone said I'd been putting mascara on in the toilets. When I pointed out that mascara went on *eyes* and this was clearly *blusher*, which went on *cheeks* so the joke was on *them*, the words were barely out of my mouth before I regretted what I'd said and the whole class fell around laughing. And when I went to the boys' toilets, everyone standing at the urinals called me a perv and accused me of trying to look at their willies. Which made no sense at all because:

FIVE REASONS WHY THIS MADE NO SENSE AT ALL

1. I'm not gay.
2. My brother Jason isn't gay.
3. Just because my brother Jason thinks he's my sister doesn't make him gay anyway.
4. Even if my brother Jason *was* gay, which he isn't, that wouldn't mean that I was gay.
5. And even if none of that was true and my brother Jason was gay, *and* I was gay, I'd still have better

things to do with my time than try to sneak a peek at their tiny, shrivelled-up little willies, which are totally gross anyway.

There'd been a lot of discussion at home a few months earlier about whether we should take a holiday during our week off, and it had proved a far more complicated decision than anyone might have expected.

'Somewhere hot,' said my brother Jason, who liked sunshine.

'Somewhere cold,' I said, who didn't.

'The weather is the least important of our concerns here,' said Mum.

'I wouldn't mind a driving holiday,' said Dad, flicking through an atlas he'd left open on the kitchen table and taking his glasses off as he ran a finger along the motorway. 'All the way from Calais to Andorra. How long do you suppose that would take? How would everyone feel about a camper van? I've always rather fancied the idea.'

'I don't think France is a very good idea,' said Mum. 'What with all the anti-European sentiment going around at the moment, the parliamentary party might think that I was making some sort of statement by going there. When the PM eventually goes, we don't want to give my enemies any unnecessary ammunition.'

'You have enemies, Mum?' I asked, looking up in concern.

'Some. No more than anyone else in my position.'

'So, Europe as a whole is out?' asked Dad. 'The entire continent?'

'Well, not necessarily,' she replied. 'We just have to be selective, that's all. It's important that I'm seen to be completely supportive of Europe while, at the same time, opposing absolutely everything it stands for.'

'I'd quite like to go to Prague,' said my brother Jason. 'I've been reading a lot of Kafka lately and they have a museum dedicated to him there.'

'Is the Czech Republic in the EU?' asked Mum.

'I think so, yes.'

'Hmm.'

'How about Italy?' asked Dad. 'The statue of David . . . the *Mona Lisa* . . .'

'The *Mona Lisa* is in Paris,' I said.

'Italy's too unstable anyway,' said Mum. 'There's always an election going on and that's the last thing I need.'

'Greece?'

'Actually, I've always wanted to see Athens,' she said, perking up a little. 'But what message does it send, do you think? That I'm offering support to them while flying in the face of EU austerity?'

'It could just mean that we got a cheap flight,' I said.

'Don't be ridiculous. Look,' she declared, raising her voice now as if she was about to make a speech in the House, and I felt a sudden urge to shout, *Order! Order! The Right Honourable Lady WILL be heard!* 'I'm not opposed to Greece and, as you all know, I bow to no one in my appreciation of feta cheese and olives, but I just think there are too many variables. It's a big world out there. Can't we think of somewhere that makes sense on every level?'

'Ireland might be nice,' I suggested.

'Well, now you're just being deliberately unhelpful,' said Mum, rolling her eyes. 'They'll accuse me of favouring a soft border. Honestly, Sam, if you're not willing to take this conversation seriously, then maybe you should just go out and play.'

'Go out and play?' I asked, wondering whether she thought I was still five years old.

'Australia?' suggested Dad.

'Too far. The flight alone would kill me.'

'Japan?'

'You know I can't stand Chinese food.'

'You do realize that China and Japan are completely different countries?' asked my brother Jason.

'How about America?' asked Dad. 'If we went to Washington, then perhaps we could –'

'Before you even begin to make some ludicrous suggestion,' said Mum, 'you need to understand that presidents only meet prime ministers, not members of another country's cabinet. But I suppose we could always get some good social media pictures that *suggest* we've been in talks with important people.'

'Is there a Disneyland in Washington?' I asked.

'Yes, it's called the White House.'

'Is there anything that Sam and I might actually like to do there?' asked my brother Jason irritably.

'Spend time with your family?' suggested Mum. 'Honestly, you boys! Your father and I take care of you throughout the year and then, the moment we propose a holiday where we can spend time together as a family, all the pair of you do is complain. I don't know why we bother, I really don't!'

In the end, we didn't even get on a plane, driving instead to the Lake District for a few days, where we went on long walks and Mum sat on rocks while Dad took pictures of her reading *The Selected Poetry of William Wordsworth* and staring off into the distance as if she wasn't quite sure who she was or what she was doing there. But when we returned to the hotel every night, the reception was always terrible, the Wi-Fi was never working, so he couldn't post them online, he ended up having a fight with the manager over a leaky shower and he declared the entire thing a complete waste of time.

From the start, though, the holiday hadn't gone well. There had been almost no discussion of what my brother Jason had told us a few months earlier and, while I wasn't surprised that Mum and Dad were refusing to talk about it, I wondered when or if he might bring it up again. It was the kind of thing that the phrase 'the elephant in the room' had been invented for, only the elephant was squashed into the back seat of the car with us, following behind whenever we went for a walk and pulling over an extra chair the moment we sat down for meals. We stuck to safe and uncontroversial subjects throughout, and I found myself veering between embarrassed frustration and a sort of bottled-up hysteria. When Dad asked me casually over dinner one night whether I'd given any thought to what I might like to do with my life when I was older, his question brought to an end a ten-minute silence around the table and I practically screamed out, 'Yes, a fireman! No, a doctor! No, a librarian! No, a carpet fitter! Or a painter and decorator! Or I could work in a zoo! Or be a vet! Maybe a fireman! No, I already said a fireman, didn't I?' In fact, I grew so frantic running through the list of every job available to me that, when I finally calmed down, everyone in the room was turned in my direction, staring at me as if I'd lost my mind. It was like I'd been discovered listening to my Ed Sheeran records again.

'Well, it's good to keep your options open anyway,' said Dad quietly as he took a sip from his pint of real ale, which he didn't like very much but thought made him look like a man of the people in photographs.

On our last night there, Mum was recognized by one of the other guests, a woman in her sixties with hair so tall and such an unnatural shade of blue that she reminded me of Marge Simpson.

'I hope you don't mind,' said the woman, coming over and extending her hand. 'You are who I think you are, aren't you?'

'Well, I suppose that depends who you think I am,' said Mum.

'The Cabinet minister? Deborah Waver, am I right?'

Mum nodded and smiled.

'I had to come over to say thank you,' said the woman. 'For all your help in getting us out. You're too young to remember, but I was one of those who protested about

Ted Heath taking us into the Common Market in the first place. Why on earth tie ourselves to a bunch of second-rate countries who eat all sorts of strange meats for breakfast and are always starting wars with each other, that's what I wanted to know. And, good Lord, most of them don't even speak *English*! Forty years we've been stuck with them, and now, finally, the nightmare is over. Thanks to people like you.'

Mum shifted in her chair, looking a little uncomfortable. 'Well, I'm not sure that's exactly how I'd define our European partners,' she said. 'And, of course, we'll still have to work with them in the –'

'It's their loss and they know it,' continued Marge Simpson. 'They all wanted to be aligned to us. What was it that Cecil Rhodes said? *Ask any man what nationality he would prefer to be and ninety-nine out of a hundred will tell you that they would prefer to be an Englishman.* He was quite right too. When the PM finally goes, I do hope you'll run for the top job. You're exactly what we need. Someone who can stand up to Johnny Foreigner!'

'At the moment there is no vacancy,' said Mum. 'So naturally I haven't even considered my own ambitions. The job now is to find a way to protect British interests while –'

'Yes, yes,' said the woman, dismissing these banalities with a wave of her hand. 'You're not on *Question Time* now, dear, there's no need for the blather. We both know where you stand. Let me tell you, over the last few years the area I live in has completely changed. My next-door neighbours – *my own next-door neighbours* – are Pakistani, if you can believe it. From somewhere near Delhi, they tell me. Or was it Seoul? One or the other. The north island, I know that much. And these days I can't even walk down the street without seeing some nancy boy trotting along hand in hand with his boyfriend. What does the Queen think, that's what I'd like to know. All those handsome young men she surrounds herself with in Buckingham Palace – the footmen and valets and so on – are any of them nancy boys? Not on your life! And you must understand, I'm the least prejudiced person you could ever meet, I even have a CD of Elton John's *Greatest Hits* in my car, but I just don't see why these people have to come and live in a community they don't fit into? They'd be happier abroad, I'm sure of it. If anything, we'd be doing them a favour.'

My parents glanced at each other with uncomfortable expressions on their faces and I could tell that Mum was about to launch into another approved party speech when my brother Jason spoke up.

'What if they object to you?' he asked.

'I beg your pardon?' said the woman, turning to look at him for the first time.

'I asked, what if they object to you?' he repeated. 'Not that they're prejudiced, of course, but what if they don't like the idea of living next to someone who feels qualified to decide who should and shouldn't live exactly where they want to?'

'Jason, stop,' said Mum.

'Is this your son?' asked Marge Simpson.

'Yes, but he doesn't know what he's talking about.'

'Why is he wearing his hair like that? He looks like Twiggy in her heyday.'

'Of course I know what I'm talking about,' said my brother Jason indignantly. 'I read the newspapers, I watch the news. I spend half my life on the internet. And my mother's a Cabinet minister, for pity's sake. I think I have *some* awareness of what's going on in the world.'

'Jason!' said Dad, raising his voice.

'What?' he asked in confusion.

'Just stop.'

'That scarf you're wearing around your neck, young man,' said the woman, leaning forward and narrowing her eyes. 'I'm sure it's designed for girls, not boys. My granddaughter has one just like it. And if you don't mind my saying so, it makes you look very feminine.'

'Thank you.'

'Why on earth is the boy thanking me?' she asked, looking around at each one of us in turn. 'It wasn't a compliment. Is he a little touched perhaps? Does he have mental issues?'

'He's fine,' said Mum. 'He's just a teenager, that's all. He's confused.'

'Oh,' said the woman dismissively. 'Well, they're a breed apart.'

'Especially the Pakistani ones,' said my brother Jason. 'And the nancy boys. Actually, historians are pretty sure that Cecil Rhodes was gay, did you know that? His lover died in his arms, in fact, and he was inconsolable afterwards. Plus, he was a white supremacist and an out-and-out racist.'

'You need to learn some manners, young man,' said the woman, shouting now and pointing a gnarly old finger at him.

'Of the two of us, I think I'm the only one who actually *has* any manners,' he replied. 'You're just an ignorant old bigot with Marge Simpson hair.'

'That's what I was thinking!' I shouted, delighted that he'd noticed the similarity too.

'Well!' she said, taking a step back and pretending to be terribly offended. 'I'm sure I didn't come over here to be insulted.'

'*Don't* say it, Sam!' barked Dad, who could see that I was all set to use one of my favourite jokes.

'I'd better not hold you up any longer,' she said, turning back to Mum. 'I can see that you've got difficulties of your own, dear. I just wanted to say thank you, that's all. And when the PM goes, you'll have my support, for what it's worth. *If* you can get your family under control before then, that is.'

'Thank you,' said Mum. 'And I do apologize for my son.'

The woman snorted a little, threw one final disgusted look at my brother Jason and disappeared back to the other side of the room.

'Don't ever apologize for me,' said my brother Jason quietly, but his voice like thunder.

'I will if you –'

'You're determined to ruin this holiday, aren't you?' asked Dad, turning to him furiously.

'I was just –'

'If you can't be polite with people, then it's best you don't open your mouth at all.'

'So I shouldn't speak?' he asked. 'I shouldn't express an opinion?'

'All things considered,' said Dad, 'it would probably be better if you didn't. And take that ridiculous scarf off and pull your hair out of that stupid ponytail. And do something about that stupid fringe and those pathetic layers that make you look like Rachel from *Friends*. Do you have any idea how embarrassing it is to be sitting next to you when you look like that?'

My brother Jason and I were sharing a bedroom, and that night, when we went upstairs, there was a real awkwardness between us, something that I'd felt deeply on the night we arrived and that had only grown in the intervening days. Before he made his big announcement, I would have loved to share a bedroom with him again, something we hadn't done since I was a little kid, but now I only felt anxious and uncomfortable. And even though he changed into his pyjamas obliviously while flicking through the channels on the television, I took mine into the bathroom and undressed in there, not even looking in his direction when I came out again.

As I climbed into bed, however, I noticed that he'd finally released his hair from the ponytail, leaving it falling around his shoulders, and that the scarf that had caused so much trouble over dinner was hanging over the back of a chair, while his blue scrunchie was sitting on the dressing table. I wondered what he'd think if he woke up and they were missing. He'd know that I had taken them, of course. But if only *one* was missing, then he might think he'd just misplaced it. Which was worse? The scarf or the scrunchie? The scarf, I decided. Definitely the scarf.

'Sam?'

I looked across to the other bed and realized that my brother Jason had been trying to get my attention.

'What's going on?' he asked. 'It's like you're in a dream world.'

'Sorry,' I said, shaking my head. 'I was just thinking of something.'

He rolled over on to his side, still looking at me as he propped his head up on one hand.

'What?'

I wondered whether to ask or not, but decided that, if I didn't do it now, I never would. 'About school,' I said.

'Yes.'

'And all the rumours.'

'What about them?'

'It must be upsetting you?'

He sighed and waited a few moments before answering. 'I'm trying to ignore the noise,' he said. 'Most of my friends have been pretty good about it, actually. Some don't know what to say. But no one has tried to bully me or anything.'

I laughed bitterly. 'Of course they haven't,' I said.

'What's that supposed to mean?'

'Well, you're *you*, aren't you?' I asked. 'If I come into school with a new spot, the whole class jumps on me. You can say that you're . . . that you're . . .'

'Transgender.'

'Yes, that. And –'

'Say it, Sam. The word isn't going to burn your mouth.'

'You can tell people that,' I continued, ignoring this, 'and no one bullies you because you've always been popular. It's so easy for people like you.'

Now it was his turn to laugh. 'You think it's easy?' he asked. 'They may not be saying mean things to my face, but do you think I don't know what they're saying behind my back? Even my closest friends are nervous of saying the wrong thing. You know there's been a few parties lately that I wasn't invited to?'

I shook my head. I didn't know that.

'A few months back, I'd have been at the top of the guest list. And now I only hear about them on Monday morning. Believe me, Sam, I may be getting a different type of response to this to you, but it's not any easier.'

I said nothing, trying to think this through. I still thought it would be easier if no one was making fun of you to your face.

'Can I ask you a question?' he asked finally.

'If you want.'

'How come you don't have many friends?'

'What?' I asked, turning to look at him in surprise.

'You never bring anyone to the house. You never go to birthday parties. You never talk about anyone from your class at school. I've been wondering for a while but wasn't sure whether to ask you or not.'

I looked away from him, towards the wardrobe, the curtains, the mirror, anywhere my eyes could alight safely without having to look at him. 'I have friends,' I replied eventually.

'I'm not trying to be mean,' he said.

'I know that.'

'I just worry about you, that's all.'

'I *have* friends,' I repeated.

'Is it because you can't read very well?' he asked.

I shrugged and took my hands out from beneath the sheet, staring at my fingers for a while. My nails needed trimming, but I hadn't thought to bring nail clippers with me on holiday. 'People think I'm stupid,' I said. 'They call me names.'

'That's what people do when they don't understand something.'

'And, because you're so good at sport and I'm so bad, people make fun of me.'

He said nothing for a while and, when he did speak, I was surprised by what he suggested.

'Do you want to raid the minibar?' he asked, and I turned to him, not sure what he meant. 'The minibar,' he repeated, jumping out of bed and opening the fridge that stood beneath the television set. It was full of small bottles and cans. 'What do you want?' he asked. 'There's Coke, Fanta, Sprite –'

'Won't we get in trouble?' I asked.

'Who cares if we do? If they didn't want us to take something from it, then they should have put a lock on the door. Here,' he said, throwing me a Fanta, and I opened it, holding it over the space between our two beds as it fizzed up. He took a can of beer and climbed back into bed with it, sipping the froth from the top and licking his lips afterwards. He wasn't supposed to be drinking beer as he was only seventeen, but I knew he liked it. Sometimes, when he came back from a night out with his friends, he was all giggly and Mum complained that he smelled like a brewery and the next day he'd lie in bed for hours and roar at me if I came anywhere near him.

'OK, Sam,' he said. 'It's ten years from now. You're twenty-three years old. Where are you?'

I thought about it. 'I have my own place,' I said.

'Good. And what else?'

'It's a really big place. Like a mansion.'

'Of course.'

'Because I'm really rich.'

'Naturally. But what are you doing?'

'Driving my sports car down the motorway with the top down and my music *blastin'*!'

'Ed Sheeran?'

'Shut up!'

'And how have you made all this money?'

I thought about it. 'I won the Lottery,' I said.

'Lucky. Have you given any to me?'

'A little. Not too much. I don't want to spoil you.'

'OK,' he said, laughing. 'Now back to real life. Seriously, where do you see yourself ten years from now?'

I shrugged my shoulders. 'I don't know,' I said. 'Am I supposed to know?'

'No,' he said, taking a spare pillow that he'd thrown on the floor earlier and propping himself up against it. 'There's no reason you should know anything yet.'

'Did you know what you wanted to be when you were my age?' I asked.

'I knew some things,' he said.

I bit my lip. I could see where this was leading and wasn't sure that I wanted to talk about it. 'All right, then,' I said. 'What about you? Ten years from now, you're twenty-seven years old. Where are you?'

'Ah,' he said, grinning and taking a long drink from his beer. 'OK. Well, first off, I'm a famous superstar writer.'

'Brilliant.'

'And every book I write sells a million copies and wins lots of awards.'

'Goes without saying.'

'And I have a beautiful girlfriend who loves me, and I love her too but she's a crazy nymphomaniac so insists on having sex with me ten times a day.'

I giggled, but then wasn't sure why I was laughing.

'What?' he asked, sensing a change in my mood.

'Nothing,' I said.

'It's not nothing. It's something. So tell me.'

'Well, it's just . . . are you sure you don't want a boy-friend?' I asked.

'Why would I want a boyfriend?'

'I don't know,' I said.

'You get that I'm not gay, right?' he asked, sounding a little frustrated. 'I mean, it would be fine if I was and I'd just come out and tell you. But I'm not.'

'Maybe you just don't know that you're gay.'

'One thing I do know is that you have a special box with a lock and key at the back of your wardrobe and it's full of old copies of Mum's *Vogue*s and the underwear issues are always on top.'

'Oh,' I said, the blood rushing to my face.

'It's OK, I don't care,' he said, laughing. 'Don't look so embarrassed, for God's sake. It's no big deal.'

'I'm not embarrassed,' I said.

'Please. If I cracked an egg on your face right now it'd be fried in about five seconds. I've got magazines like that too. And I know you've found them because you snoop around my room too. And what do you see in them? The ones in my room, I mean.'

'Girls,' I said.

'Exactly. Girls. Ever seen any boys?'

'Well, sometimes,' I told him. 'But they're always with the girls. Like, doing things with them.'

'I don't buy them for the boys,' he said. 'I buy them because Mum and Dad won't take the parental controls off our computers.'

'I know,' I said. 'I hate that.'

'So I'm not gay.'

'OK.'

'I'm *not*!'

'I believe you,' I said, growing irritated now. 'But if you think you're really a girl, then shouldn't that mean you want to be with boys?'

'Not necessarily,' he said. 'It's very complicated.'

'Then tell me,' I said, turning to him now. 'Because I don't understand what's going on. Explain it to me.'

He sat back and sighed before taking another long drink from his beer, finishing it, and getting another.

'Do you know what one of my first memories is?' he asked, and I shook my head. 'I was three years old and I'd just started at that playschool we used to go to when we were little – do you remember it?'

'Yes,' I said. I'd spent a year there too before starting real school. It was full of screaming kids and more Lego than I'd ever seen before or since. I'd really enjoyed it.

'It was my first day,' he said. 'And I was playing with a girl called Amelia and a boy called Jack. And Amelia said she needed a wee, so then Jack said he needed a wee, so naturally I said I needed a wee too, so all three of us got up to go to the toilets, and there were two, of course, one for the boys and one for the girls, but they were next door to each other. And when we reached them, Jack went one way and Amelia went the other. But I followed her. She screamed – even though we'd barely got inside the door – and pushed me out, and the teacher came over and told me that I'd gone to the wrong door, that the boys' was over there, and I shook my head and refused to go in. No matter what she did, I said I wouldn't use it, that I was supposed to go to the girls' toilet. And, you know, I was only about three years old. I didn't know anything about anything. But it just felt . . . right to me to go to the girls'. In the end, because she wouldn't let me in there, I wet myself and all the other kids were laughing and pointing at me. I didn't care so much about that. There was barely an hour went by when someone in that room wasn't wetting themselves for one reason or another. By the end of most days it was like we'd all gone down on the *Titanic*. Anyway, Mum and Dad were called in the next morning and they told me off, and from then on, every time I had to go, I had to use the boys' room, but from that day to this it has just never felt right.'

'You always use the disabled toilet,' I said quietly, remembering something I'd noticed for a few years but never thought much about. I just thought he was self-conscious.

'I do, yeah,' he said. 'I can't go into the girls', obviously. But I just don't feel right about going to the boys' either.'

'So that's it?' I asked, thinking that this didn't seem like much of a reason. 'That's why you think you're a girl?'

'No, of course not. It's just the first thing I remember, that's all. But my entire life has been built around moments like that. Asking for a doll for Christmas and being told no, I had to have a toy gun or a computer game. Being taken shopping for new clothes and just feeling that I was in the wrong part of the store, that a magnet was pulling me to the next floor up. You probably won't remember this, but when I was about twelve I had a birthday party, and for the first time I didn't want to invite *any* boys to it. Just the girls. I was at that stage where I hated boys. And Dad kept calling me Casanova, but he had it all wrong. Everyone's bodies were changing and I felt like I belonged with the girls, not the boys. Does that make any sense to you?'

I said nothing.

'Think about it, Sam,' he said. 'You're thirteen years old now. If four people from your class came over to the house and spent an afternoon with you in your bedroom, who would you feel more comfortable around? Four boys or four girls?'

'Four boys,' I said.

'And yet you like looking at pictures of girls with very few clothes on. Which is how it is for most people your age. But I was always just different. I wanted to be with girls *and* look at girls.'

'So . . . do you mean you *are* gay?' I asked.

'I already told you –'

'No, I mean, if you think you're really a girl but you like girls, doesn't that show that you *are* gay after all? Like a gay girl?'

'Well, I suppose,' he said, thinking about this. 'I don't know. That's where it gets really complicated. I still have to figure that one out. I don't know all the answers yet, Sam. I'm only seventeen. I'm still trying to understand all this myself. It's really difficult.'

'And what about football?'

'I just happen to *like* football!' he said. 'And I'm good at it! Lots of girls are, you know!'

'The thing is,' I said, after taking a few moments to think about all this, 'I hated it when you said you weren't my brother.'

'Maybe I phrased it wrong,' he said. 'One thing I know for sure, though, is that you're *my* brother. And that you always will be.'

'But you're a *boy*,' I insisted.

'If you tell me one more time that I have a willy, I'm going to start thinking you're the one who's gay.'

The whole thing was becoming too puzzling for me and I definitely couldn't joke about it, so I climbed out of bed and went into the bathroom. Once inside I stared into the mirror and looked at my face. I was a boy, wasn't I? I touched my cheeks and chin. I felt above my upper lip for any sign of a moustache, which I was hoping was going to kick in any day now. I looked inside my pyjama bottoms. *I was a boy!* If my brother Jason could suddenly change, then could I? Because I didn't want to.

A knock on the door.

'Sam?' he asked. 'Sam, are you OK?'

'I'm fine,' I said.

'Then come out.'

'I'm in the toilet.'

'Yes, but you're not *going* to the toilet, so come out. Please.'

I waited a few moments and then unlocked the door, leaping quickly from the bathroom into my bed and pulling the sheets up to my chin.

'All right,' he said with a sigh, walking slowly back to his bed and getting in. 'Tell me what you're most frightened of.'

I swallowed. 'What if it happens to me?' I asked.

'What do you mean?'

'What if I wake up one day and think I'm a girl?'

My brother Jason laughed and shook his head. 'Trust me, you won't.'

'How do you know?'

'I just know.'

'Because I don't want to be a girl,' I insisted, feeling tears spring up behind my eyes. 'I hate girls –'

'You don't hate girls.'

'No, but I don't want to be one. They dress stupid and wear perfume and are always dancing and rolling their eyes at everyone and being mean and talking about Justin Bieber and –'

'Oh, for God's sake, Sam,' he said irritably. 'There's a lot more to girls than that. Stop being such a dick.'

'What?'

He sighed. 'Honestly, Sam, you don't have anything to worry about. If there's one thing I know for sure, it's that you and I are not alike on this. You're a boy and you always will be.'

'I'm tired,' I said. 'I just want to go to sleep. Can we go to sleep? I don't want to talk about this any more.'

'You don't hate me, though, do you?'

'Of course I don't hate you,' I said. 'I just want you to get better, that's all.'

'*To get better?*' He sat up in bed and stared at me with an expression of such disbelief on his face that I wondered what I'd said wrong. 'Did you just say that you want me to get *better*?'

'Yes. What's wrong with that?'

'So you think I'm sick, is that it? That I've got an illness of some kind?'

I said nothing for a moment. I knew what I was supposed to say and what he wanted to hear, but I didn't care. 'Well, that's what Mum and Dad say,' I told him, knowing as I said this that I was being unfair passing the blame on to them.

'All right,' he said eventually. 'Well, I'm sorry you feel that way.'

'Will you turn the light off?' I asked, lying down and turning my back on him.

'Not just yet,' he said. 'Close your eyes if you're tired. You'll be asleep soon enough.'

And I did what he said. I closed my eyes, and after a few minutes I changed the sound of my breathing to make it seem that I was asleep. But the problem with pretending to be asleep is that you can't look up when you hear someone opening another beer, and another, and another after that, and then falling down into the bed to the sound of their tears, and you have to wait until they've finally fallen asleep before you can get up and turn off all the lights. And you don't get a chance to say sorry.

4

Goldfish and Kangaroos

My nemesis, David Fugue, was boring us all to death with the story of how his father's business partner's sister's next-door neighbour's cousin had recently spent a weekend with Harry and Meghan when a knock came on the classroom door and the school secretary, Mrs Flynn, stepped inside.

'Sorry to disturb, Mr Lowry,' she said, glancing around the room. 'But Sam Waver is to gather his things and come to reception with me. His parents are waiting for him.'

This unexpected summons led to cries and whistles from the entire class, who, enjoying any disruption to their usual routine, wondered aloud whether I was being expelled, arrested or put up for adoption.

'Maybe he's getting fitted for his first training bra,' shouted David Fugue, and I threw him a furious look. 'Or do you just take your brother's when he's outgrown them?'

'Shut up,' I snapped at him.

'Oh, watch out, he's on his period,' said David, doubling over with laughter, and now I jumped out of my seat and was about to launch myself at him, hands curled into fists, only Mr Lowry leaped between us in time – which, to be fair, I was counting on. My days of invisibility were over. Everyone could see me now.

'Just get your bag and coat, Sam,' he said calmly. 'And go with Mrs Flynn.'

'Next time, Fugue,' I said, stabbing a finger in the air in his direction. 'Next time!'

'Yeah? What are you going to do? Hit me with your handbag?'

'That's enough, David!' shouted Mr Lowry, spinning round and glaring at him. 'One more word out of you and –'

'I didn't say anything, sir!' said David, holding his hands up as if he couldn't believe the injustice of the accusation.

I collected my belongings, my face red with a mixture of embarrassment and anger, and made my way to the door, following Mrs Flynn down the corridor with the sound of laughter trailing behind me. For a while, I told myself, I had been getting along fine in school, nowhere near the top of the popularity list but with no serious enemies either, and now I was a figure of fun to everyone. And none of it, *none of it*, was my fault.

I still wasn't sure what was going on, but when I arrived at reception, where Mum and Dad were waiting for me, I rolled my eyes as soon as I saw that my brother Jason was wearing his long hair in a ponytail again, this time with a red scrunchie since his blue one had mysteriously gone missing while we were on holiday, along with the girly scarf, and for a moment I wondered whether we were both being taken out of school forever and sent somewhere different, where no one knew either of us. Hogwarts, maybe. Where I could magic him back into the way he used to be.

'What kept you?' asked Mum, glancing at her watch.

'What's going on?' I asked, irritated by her question, for I'd come as soon as I'd been called. 'What are you doing here?'

'We have an appointment,' said Dad. 'All of us.'

Three boys from the Second XI football team, the ones who weren't quite good enough to play with the Firsts, passed by, and when they saw us they started laughing.

'Faggot,' muttered one under his breath but loud enough for us to hear.

'Peter Hopkins, what did you just say?' asked Mrs Flynn, turning round, but he simply shrugged and walked on, ignoring her. As school secretary she couldn't issue detentions so struggled to have the same level of authority over us as the other adults.

'So they all know?' asked Mum, turning to my brother Jason.

'Know what?' he asked. 'He said *faggot* and, since I'm not gay, I don't know what you mean by so *they all know?*'

'You know exactly what I mean,' said Mum. 'Please don't try to be smart.'

'We're in a school,' he said. 'That's the whole point of the place.'

'Enough,' said Dad, raising his voice. 'Come on, we've wasted enough time as it is. The car's outside.'

'But where are we going?' I asked, and as I made my way towards the door I walked past the sequence of football-team photographs that stretched all the way back to before the First World War, where the boys wore haunted expressions and had dark, unhappy eyes, as if they knew their lives were about to be cut short. I'd always been fascinated by these pictures; they made me feel very sad. When I reached the last one, however, I saw my brother Jason seated in the centre of the front row.

Someone had drawn a dress on him in red marker.

Outside, Bradley was holding the back door of the ministerial car open and Mum, Dad and I jumped into the back seat, while my brother Jason went round to the other side and climbed into the passenger seat. Mum had been a Cabinet minister since the last election two years earlier and Bradley had been her driver ever since. When she was in a good mood, she chatted away to him as if they were best friends, but when she wasn't, she treated him as if she was barely aware of his existence, and I suspected that, while he was always polite, he didn't have a particularly high opinion of her. He got along best with my brother Jason, for they were both football fans, although on opposite sides of the London divide – Chelsea and Arsenal – and whenever they were in each other's company they could talk about it endlessly.

'You have the address, Bradley?' asked Mum as she took out her phone and began checking her emails.

'Yes,' he replied. 'I'll have you there in twenty minutes, give or take.'

'Bradley,' said Dad, leaning forward between the seats, 'I presume I don't have to tell you that this is a private –'

'I'll have you there in twenty minutes, Mr Waver,' repeated Bradley, pulling out on to the road, and Dad hovered for a moment before sitting back and staring out of the window.

'Will someone please tell me where we're going?' I asked, glancing at my watch. There were still another two classes left of school and I'd been quite looking forward to maths, because the results of a recent test were due back to us that day. I'm quite good at maths, because it doesn't involve a lot of words, and I thought I might have got an 'A'.

'Have you seen what Simon's said about the build-up of nuclear weapons along the Russian seaboard?' muttered Mum as she scanned her iPad with her free hand.

'I saw it,' said Dad. 'Did he clear the text with you in advance?'

'Well, he sent it through to the office, yes. I wouldn't go so far as to say that he actually "cleared it" with me, though. I think he's trying to bring Rachel and Bobby out into the open on this and see where they stand. Joe was in quickly with a rebuttal.'

'Are we going home?' I asked. 'Has something happened?'

'Joe's trying to strike out on his own,' said Dad. 'He's seeing whether there'll be any support for him when the moment comes.'

'And do you think there will be?'

'We'll know in a couple of hours.'

'Next year will be interesting,' said my brother Jason to Bradley. 'If things keep going as they have been for Chelsea, you'll be able to visit all those Championship grounds you've never seen before. That'll be a nice treat for you.'

'Cheeky sod,' said Bradley, laughing. 'I expect you'll be hoping for a strong fourth-place finish as usual? It's good not to have ambitions. Saves your lot from getting too disappointed.'

'This isn't the way home,' I said, looking out of the window and seeing Green Park Tube station pass us by.

'More on the health crisis on page seven of the *Guardian*,' said Mum.

'I've heard a rumour that the Lewis Report will be out next Thursday,' said Dad, pulling his own phone out of his pocket and scanning through it.

I gave up asking questions since I might as well not even have been in the car – my cloak of invisibility might have been taken away from me at school, but around my family nothing seemed to have changed – and just stared out of the window, looking at girls whenever we stopped at a set of traffic lights. The ministerial car's windows were blacked out so I could stare for as long as I liked and they wouldn't know.

Soon enough we were driving through a part of London that was completely unfamiliar to me, and before long we pulled up outside a block of tall red-brick buildings that looked as if they'd been there for hundreds of years.

'Here we are, Secretary of State,' said Bradley, and both Mum and Dad let out deep sighs as they unbuckled their seat belts, as if they'd secretly hoped we'd never arrive. Like I always did when I was taken to the dentist.

'We shouldn't be more than an hour,' said Dad.

'I can't park here,' said Bradley. 'But I'll find somewhere nearby – just call me when you're ready for the pick-up.'

'Can't you stick the ministerial tag on,' asked Mum, 'and just stay put?'

'I can,' he said slowly. 'If you want me to. But as we're not here on official business I'd have to explain why to any traffic warden who happens to pass by. So it's up to you.'

There was a long silence as Mum and Dad looked at each other and frowned. 'Best to keep circling,' said Dad finally. 'We'll see you around four o'clock.'

Mum, Dad and I stepped out of the car, and only when we were on the street did I realize that my brother Jason was still inside, staring directly ahead and not looking at us. I glanced around, wondering where we were, but nothing here seemed familiar to me.

'Jason,' said Mum, knocking on the car window, 'come on.'

He continued staring ahead, saying nothing.

'Jason!' she snapped. 'I'm not going to ask twice. Bradley, can you do something please?' she asked in her most frustrated tone, appealing to our driver, but he simply shrugged.

'I don't have an ejector seat,' he said. 'It's not a bloody James Bond movie.'

'Jason,' roared Dad, knocking on the window so ferociously that I worried the glass might break, even though Bradley had told me once that it was bulletproof. 'Get out here right now.'

At last he gave in, unclipped his seat belt and opened the door.

'Fine,' he said. 'But, for the record, I want to make it clear that I don't want to be here and that I'm only agreeing to come under protest.'

'And, for the record,' said Mum, 'I don't care. Now come on. You never know who might be watching a place like this.'

We walked up the steps and, before Dad could even ring the bell, the door opened, revealing a woman of about sixty with grey hair and thick-framed glasses. She looked like one of the grannies from the Shreddies ads.

'Secretary of State,' she said, smiling as she extended her hand. 'Won't you come in?'

'Please, just call me Mrs Waver,' said Mum, dismissing the title that I knew she usually enjoyed.

'Of course,' said the woman, closing the door behind us.

'I have to be very careful, you know,' said Mum. 'If this were to leak –'

'Mrs Waver, you really don't need to worry about that,' said the woman, looking at Mum with an expression on her face that suggested that if she'd ever thought of voting for her in the past, she wouldn't do it now. 'No one knows that you're here and no one will. We're a highly professional organization and I can assure you that you're not the only high-profile client who has walked through these doors and you won't be the last.'

'Really?' asked Dad. 'Why, who else comes? Anyone on the political front?'

'Mr Waver, I obviously can't say.'

'Oh, go on. We won't tell anyone.'

She ignored him and led the way down a corridor with a thick carpet under our feet and boring old paintings of hills and mountains on the walls. The smell of scented candles wafted through the air and pan-pipe music was playing. It felt as we were in the lift of a luxury hotel.

'If you'd just like to wait here,' said the woman, opening the door to a large room, and we stepped inside, 'the doctor will be with you in a few minutes.'

I walked over to a side table where a solitary goldfish was swimming in circles in a glass bowl. No one had bothered to put any stones or miniature trees inside to give him something to look at and I thought that was a bit mean. I pressed my face up close to the bowl and stared at him, but he seemed uninterested, moving through the water with an urgency that suggested he was deeply concerned about being late for an appointment.

'How can you tell if goldfish are boys or girls?' I asked, turning round and looking at my parents.

'Is this a joke?' asked Dad. 'I don't know, how can you tell if goldfish are boys or girls?'

'It's not a joke,' I said. 'It's an actual question. Because goldfish don't have willies.'

'Must you always be talking about boy bits and girl bits?' asked Mum, looking up at me irritably. 'Honestly, it's like an obsession with you.'

'It's his age,' said Dad. 'It's perfectly normal.'

'It must be good to have a normal child,' said my brother Jason.

'Oh, don't start,' said Mum, rolling her eyes. 'Or at least wait until we're inside. Then you can blame us for everything that's gone wrong with you.'

'I didn't know anything *had* gone wrong with me,' he replied.

'I wonder if they just have sex with each other and hope for the best,' I said. 'Maybe they don't even care whether they're doing it with a boy or a girl.'

'There's a few of those on the back benches,' muttered Mum.

'The vote's been moved back to seven thirty,' said Dad, whose phone had just pinged. 'That gives us some breathing room anyway.'

'Good,' said Mum. 'I want to take the temperature of the party before committing to anything.'

'The boys chase the girls,' said my brother Jason, turning to me. 'They can tell instinctively who's who and what's what. And they bump into the ones they like. Then the girls get so freaked out, they drop their eggs and the boys fertilize them.'

'Oh,' I said. 'How do you know that?'

'I read about it somewhere,' he said with a shrug of his shoulders.

'Where are we anyway?' I asked. 'Why are we at a doctor's office? Is someone sick?'

'Me, apparently,' said my brother Jason.

'He's not physically sick,' said Dad. 'But obviously there are . . . psychological issues. We thought that, as a family, we should speak to someone and get some help.'

'Oh,' I said. 'So this is a psychiatrist's office?'

'A psychologist's,' said Mum.

'What's the difference?'

Before she could answer, the door opened and the granny from the Shreddies ad popped her head in again.

'Sorry for the delay,' she said, 'but Dr Watson can see you now.'

I burst out laughing. 'Dr Watson?' I asked.

'That's right,' she said, turning to me, her smile fading instantly. 'Dr John Watson. What's so amusing about that?'

'Dr *John* Watson?' I roared.

'Yes. Is that amusing to you in some way?'

'Well . . . you know,' I said, feeling my face grow a little red. 'Sherlock Holmes? Dr John Watson. It's just . . . I thought it was funny, that's all.'

'I don't see why,' said the woman, looking utterly affronted. 'Dr Watson is one of the most eminent men in his field. You have no business mocking him.'

'All right,' I said, suitably chastised. 'Sorry.'

'Also, your fly is undone. You might want to zip it up.'

I looked down and, sure enough, it was. Had it been like that all day, I wondered, and, if so, why had nobody bothered to tell me? Sometimes it felt as if no one even knew I was in the room.

Based on television shows I'd seen, I expected Dr Watson to be an elderly man with a Sigmund Freud beard and a tweed jacket with leather patches on the elbows, for his office to be filled with books from floor to ceiling and for it to look like no one had cleaned it since the late nineteenth century. But, to my surprise, he was quite young, no more than thirty-five, and dressed as if he was on the way to the pub with his friends. He looked a lot like the singer from Coldplay.

'It's very nice to meet you all,' he said, indicating a sofa and two chairs opposite his own. Mum and Dad took the sofa; my brother Jason and I took the chairs.

'I'm sure you're feeling a little nervous about talking to a stranger about such personal matters, but let me assure you that this is a safe place where there are no judgements and everything that's said within these four walls will remain completely confidential.'

'I'm glad you've brought that up,' said Dad, reaching for his briefcase and pulling out a folder that held a document containing six or seven pages. 'I actually have something here that I need you to sign before we go any further. It just keeps us all covered in case of leaks. It's quite standard, of course. There's nothing unusual in there. If you can just initial each page here, here and here and then sign at the end. Also, I need to take a photograph of you while you're signing it.'

'I'm afraid I can't do that,' said Dr Watson, flicking through the pages for a moment before handing them back. 'I don't engage in legal declarations with clients. We have to operate from a position of trust if we're to have any success at all. But of course you understand that I'm bound by the Hippocratic oath, right? I'd be struck off if I revealed anything that was spoken about in here.'

'I understand that,' said Dad, looking unconvinced. 'But, still, we would feel a lot safer if –'

'It's fine,' said Mum, interrupting him and shaking

her head. 'He's a doctor. Of course he'll keep things confidential.'

'Did anyone ever tell you that you're the image of Chris Martin?' asked my brother Jason, and Dr Watson nodded.

'I get that a lot,' he said. 'But I can't sing.'

'Well, neither can he. Are you going to try to fix me?'

He made quotation marks in the air with his fingers when he said to *fix me*, just like Mum had done when she'd used the word *transgender*. I thought about pointing this out but decided I better not.

'Do you like music, Jason?' asked Dr Watson after a moment's pause, during which I stifled a snigger and my brother smiled.

'Oh, we've started already, have we?' he asked. 'Subtle.'

'No,' he replied, shaking his head and laughing. 'Not really. It was just a question, that's all.' He looked around at us all. 'So,' he said, bringing his hands together for a moment, 'why don't you tell me what brought you here today.'

There was a long silence. Mum and Dad both looked uncertain how to respond, while my brother Jason was sitting with his arms wrapped around himself and I wasn't sure anyway.

Finally, Mum spoke.

'We have a small problem, Doctor,' she said. 'Our son Jason is going through some sort of identity crisis.'

Another long silence.

'All right,' said Dr Watson. 'And how has this identity crisis manifested itself?'

'He's gone insane,' said Dad.

Dr Watson smiled. 'Perhaps we can leave the clinical definitions to those of us with medical degrees,' he said. 'Jason, why don't you tell me what they're referring to.'

'You can probably tell just by looking at me.'

'What makes you think that?'

'Because of my hair,' he replied. 'And the fact that I'm wearing mascara.'

'This is a new thing,' said Dad. 'The make-up, I mean. This has just started today.'

'I'm wearing mascara because I was going out,' said my brother Jason defiantly. 'I had a shower too and combed my hair.'

'Yes, I can see that. But I'd still prefer it if you put it into actual words. The way you present yourself is neither here nor there to me.'

'All right,' he said, looking towards the window and taking a long time to reply. When he did, he spoke quite carefully, his voice low, and I knew that he was weighing up the meaning of every phrase before saying it, wanting each one to express exactly what he was thinking. 'I was born a boy, but for as long as I can remember I've believed that there was some sort of mistake made. By God, or whoever. It's as if the body I have is not the one I'm supposed to have. The truth is, I've always believed that I'm actually a girl. I've bottled those feelings up all my life and never spoken about them until recently. I was frightened to talk about them, I suppose. Frightened for what it might mean. But somehow I just don't feel that sense of panic any more. I want to understand it. I want to discover how to be the "me" that I think I am and be able to live my life the way I'm supposed to. Right now, every day I spend as Jason feels like twenty-four hours of dishonesty. And I don't want to be a dishonest person.'

'You see?' asked Dad, throwing his hands in the air and then tapping the side of his head repeatedly with his finger, like a woodpecker attacking a tree. 'Crazy! Completely loop the loop!'

'Mr and Mrs Waver,' said the doctor, 'perhaps it would be better if I spoke to Jason alone. Phrases like that are really unhelpful.'

'No,' said Mum defiantly. 'No, it's important that

we're part of this. I want to understand. And so does my husband. He didn't mean what he just said. Apologize, Alan.'

'Sorry,' said Dad, a little chastened.

'It's just that Jason might feel he can talk more freely if –'

'Doctor, no offence,' said Mum, looking him directly in the eye, 'but he's our son. And, no matter how we feel about all this, we want to be part of it, all right? We *have* to be part of it.'

I noticed how my brother Jason looked across at her then and the hostility on his face disappeared. Instead, he gave a half-smile and Mum did too, and she even looked as if she might reach out and take his hand, but that didn't happen.

'Thank you,' he said. 'It's important to me that you are. That's why I told you so early. I can't do this without you.'

'But it's the fact that you feel you have to do it at all,' she said quietly, looking as if she might cry.

'Jason,' said Dr Watson, after a lengthy pause, his tone just as measured as my brother's. I liked his voice; there was something very calming about it. 'You're seventeen years old and you're working through some very serious issues. I think we can all agree – I think *you* can agree – that, at the very least, you might need some guidance moving forward.'

'Well, I suppose so,' he agreed.

'Could there be some sort of childhood trauma behind all this?' asked Mum. 'We used to have a lot of au pairs and maybe one of them . . . I don't know . . . *did* something to him. And he's blocked it out of his mind. Maybe you can get him to uncover those memories? Hypnosis, maybe? And once he gets it all out, then all this will go away and we can get back to normal.'

'Do you watch a lot of films, Mrs Waver?' asked Dr Watson.

'Not really,' said Mum, looking a little surprised by the question. 'I saw that one about Winston Churchill a couple of months ago. And the one where Meryl Streep played Mrs Thatcher. Obviously my job keeps me very busy and I don't get the opportunity to go to the cinema very often. Why do you ask?'

'Because that's the sort of thing that happens mostly in films,' he replied, 'but not so much in real life.'

'Well,' replied Mum, looking at Dad as if she was expecting him to defend her, 'I don't know if that's true.'

'The thing is, your focus seems to be very much on turning Jason back into the boy he used to be,' continued Dr Watson. 'As if there's something wrong with him that we can fix. Wouldn't it be better to accept that he knows his own mind and feels this is the right decision for him?'

Mum took a long time to answer, and when she did her voice was very quiet. 'I suppose so,' she admitted. 'I just worry about how difficult his life might be. There's a lot of prejudice out there. Do I want a bunch of drunken yobs to beat him up some night just because they're too insecure themselves to let others be who they want to be?'

'Of course not.'

'I'm trying to be the best mother I know how to be,' she continued, raising her voice now. 'I'm doing what I feel is right for him. I just don't want him to suffer, that's all.'

No one spoke for a few minutes as we took this in, and I got the impression that the doctor wanted us all to take in Mum's words. She was crying a little, and when Dad offered her a hanky she waved it away and wiped her cheeks dry with the back of her hand before turning to look out of the window, staring into the street beyond.

'Jason mentioned his hair,' said Dad tentatively. 'I find it quite embarrassing when he wears it in a ponytail like that. It makes him look very feminine.'

'Thank you,' said my brother Jason.

'And, as you can see, he insists on wearing mascara. What's next? Lipstick? Perfume? High heels and a cocktail dress?'

I sat bolt upright as I remembered the Very Strange Afternoon when I'd come home from school early and my brother Jason had made me go downstairs to my mother's office without coming into the kitchen. And afterwards I'd smelled perfume in the air and seen a trace of lipstick on his face and assumed that he'd had a girl in the house. Now it all made sense. He must have thought he had the house to himself for a few hours and was dressing up.

'People stare at him,' added Mum, leaning forward now and touching the doctor on the arm. 'And then they look at us and I know exactly what they're thinking.'

'What are they thinking?' asked Dr Watson.

'They're thinking, *I blame the parents*.'

'Blame you for what?'

'For what he's turned into.'

'And what has he turned into? In your view?'

'A different person,' said Dad.

'And is that what's important here? How people look at you?'

'Yes,' said Dad. 'No. Oh, I don't know. It's impossible

for me to think up the right answers on the spur of the moment.'

'I don't want the *right answers*,' said Dr Watson, and now it was his turn to give the air quotes. 'I just want honesty, that's all.'

'And that's what I'm trying to give you. Do I want my son to be bullied? No, of course not. My wife has already expressed that. Do I think this reflects on me in some way? I wouldn't be human if I pretended it didn't. Can't you at least allow that I have the right to my own feelings?'

'As they affect you, yes. But are they the most important thing?'

Dad shook his head, not willing to consider this. 'Is there a course of antibiotics that you could give him, perhaps? We wondered whether electroshock therapy might still be a thing and whether you think it gets results? We're open to anything, even if there's a little discomfort involved.'

'For what it's worth,' said Dr Watson, turning to my brother, 'I like your hair. But, as you can see, I'm going thin on top so I'm probably jealous.'

'Please don't encourage him,' said Mum irritably. 'I know musicians think that anything goes –'

'But I'm not a musician,' he said. 'I'm not actually Chris Martin.'

'I meant psychologists. I'm sorry, but the resemblance is so strong it's a little unsettling. I know *psychologists* think that anything goes, but I don't think it's helpful if we encourage him.'

'But you've always encouraged me in things before,' said Jason. 'With football, for example.'

'That's different.'

'And you encourage Sam with his reading difficulties.'

'Also different.'

'You're actually more encouraging than you give yourselves credit for,' continued my brother Jason, his tone softening now. 'I know you want to get to the top of the greasy pole but, for the most part, you're really good parents. You praise us when we get good results, you don't go mad when we don't. You've always listened to the things we say, and no one's ever hit us, except Dad when he rolls up the newspapers and whacks us on the head with them. Don't you realize that, when I came downstairs that night to talk to you, it was because I trusted you? I was sure that you'd understand and would help me. You're not the ones going through the difficulties here, I am.'

I glanced at my parents and no one said anything for

a while. Mum was looking at my brother Jason with an expression of love on her face, combined with total confusion, and a moment later she wiped some tears from her eyes. Dad took her hand and looked at the floor, and he started tapping his foot nervously.

'We're trying to help you,' said Mum finally. 'But is it so wrong that we don't want you to turn yourself into a girl?'

'I'm not turning myself into a girl,' he insisted. 'I *am* a girl.'

'You're not!' insisted Dad. 'You're a boy. And we don't want you to do something now that might have a negative effect on your life in the future. There can be some very thoughtless people out there.'

'There can be some very thoughtless people in here,' muttered my brother Jason.

'That's not fair!' cried Mum, looking back at him. Her eyes were very red now and she looked like she always looked during hay-fever season. 'We're trying. Can't you at least give us some credit for that?'

'You say these feelings have always been with you,' said Dr Watson, turning to my brother Jason. 'Can you tell us a little more about that?'

We all looked at him now and, once again, it took him a long time to reply. 'When I was a child,' he said eventually, 'I was more drawn to girls' toys than to boys'. I wanted a doll's house for Christmas, but Mum and Dad wouldn't let me have one.'

'That never happened,' said Mum, looking away.

'Yes it did,' he insisted. 'I begged for one for weeks, and you said that if I asked one more time then I'd get nothing at all because Santa didn't come to boys who asked for girls' things. I think I was about five at the time.'

More silence. Mum and Dad stared at him, their jaws set firm, but said nothing.

'Go on,' said Dr Watson.

'And even the books I wanted to read were different. I wanted *Nancy Drew,* and instead I was given *The Hardy Boys.* In school, I preferred the company of girls, I felt safer among them, as if that was where I belonged. But, of course, I couldn't be with them all the time. I had to be with the boys. But I never felt like I belonged there.'

'But I understand that you're very physically active? That you're captain of your football team?'

'I am, yes,' he said. 'But what does that have to do with anything?'

'I mention it only because, traditionally, football is considered a masculine pursuit.'

'So is politics,' he replied, 'but look at Mum. Should

she not have been ambitious because she's a woman? Of course not! And she's become a Cabinet minister with her eye on the top job.'

'Not strictly true,' said Mum quickly, looking directly at Dr Watson. 'After all, there's no vacancy at the moment and, while one would never seek advancement for one's own sake, if one's colleagues were to –'

'I just happen to *like* football,' continued my brother Jason, interrupting her. 'And I'm good at it too. I'm the best in my class, everyone says so. I shouldn't have to justify that.'

'Arsenal Academy wanted to sign him up,' said Dad. 'He refused.'

'I couldn't,' said my brother Jason, and I could see that he was becoming emotional now, for there was a crack in his voice and he was looking down at the floor rather than at any of us. 'That whole atmosphere . . . I couldn't have done it. *They* wanted me to do it – Mum and Dad, I mean. They said it would be good for Mum's career if I became a professional footballer.'

'You make it sound like we wanted it for our own sake,' said Mum. 'We were only thinking of you. Professional footballers earn a lot of money. And you love football! We were trying to encourage you in something that was your passion.'

'Please, Mrs Waver,' said Dr Watson, interrupting her. 'Let Jason speak.'

'I'm not stopping him,' she muttered, sounding like a child who had just been scolded.

'Anyway, there's no law saying that girls can't play football,' he continued. 'When we play matches, they all come to watch. And, you know, in the States, more women play football than men. Look, it just happens to be the sport I like, and what's wrong with that? I have no interest in . . . I don't know . . . netball or whatever. Things that we usually associate with girls. And just because I feel I'm a girl doesn't mean I have to like *everything* girls like, does it? Dad watches ballroom-dancing shows. Mum likes documentaries about construction workers. I just don't think we should get hung up on the fact that I happen to like football. It's just gender stereotyping.'

'He'll have picked that phrase up from the internet,' said Mum, rolling her eyes. 'He's very modern, as you can tell.'

Dr Watson nodded slowly, considering this, before sitting back in his chair and glancing in my direction.

'In a way,' he said, addressing Mum and Dad, 'I'm surprised that you brought Sam with you today.'

'Why?' asked Mum. 'He's part of the family.'

'No, it's a good thing, certainly,' he replied. 'We don't want him to feel excluded from the changes that are going on at home. But did you ask Jason whether he wanted Sam to be included?'

'They didn't even ask me whether *I* wanted to be included,' said my brother Jason.

Dr Watson thought about that and scribbled something on a pad of paper before turning to me. 'How old are you, Sam?'

'Thirteen,' I said.

'And do you understand what we're talking about here? What your brother is saying? The things he's feeling?'

I gave a non-committal nod. 'Yes,' I said. 'Sort of. I think so. Not really. No.'

'And how does it make you feel?'

I said nothing for a long time. I didn't want to be mean but I didn't want to be dishonest either.

'Sam, how does it make you feel?' he asked again.

'I don't like it,' I said.

'Why not?'

'Because he's my big brother. And now he says he wants to be my big sister. And I don't want a big sister.'

'Actually, we're very worried about the effect all this is having on Sam,' said Mum. 'What if he wakes up one day and says he wants to be . . . I don't know . . . a kangaroo or something?'

'Oh, for God's sake!' shouted my brother Jason. 'It's hardly the same thing. I don't want to be a kangaroo. I'm saying that, inside myself, I believe I'm a girl, that's all! And you're comparing that to someone wanting to be an animal? Do you know how that makes me –'

'Jason, don't talk to your mother like that,' said Dad.

'I'm not comparing you to an animal,' said Mum. 'All right, that was a bad choice of words. I apologize. But you must admit, to say that you want to be a girl when you are quite clearly a boy –'

'He has a willy.'

'– is the most ridiculous –'

'I told you I didn't want to be here,' said my brother Jason, standing up in a rage before marching towards the door. 'You're not even listening to a word I'm saying.'

'I think they *are* listening, Jason,' said Dr Watson. 'But you have to hear them out too.'

'No, they're just insulting me. I'm sorry, Doctor, but I have to go.'

'Maybe we could talk another time, Jason?' he asked. 'Just the two of us? That would be all right, wouldn't it, Mrs Waver? Mr Waver?'

Mum and Dad both nodded. 'Of course,' Mum said.

'If that would be better. We just want to help and to understand and –'

But my brother Jason had gone, slamming the door behind him.

We all sat in silence after he left and I glanced at my watch. I wanted to go home. I wanted to lie on my bed, close my eyes and pretend that none of this was happening.

'You never answered my question regarding the electroshock therapy,' said Dad eventually, turning back to Dr Watson. 'Tell me, is that something that still goes on?'

5

The Ponytail

In the end, it didn't matter how much my brother Jason liked playing football or how good he was at it; he decided to leave the team anyway. Coach O'Brien came to our house one evening, looking like he'd rather bore a hole to the centre of the earth with his tongue than have the conversation he'd come there to have.

I'd never liked Coach O'Brien very much. Because my brother Jason was so good at sport, he expected me to be good too, but I could barely kick a ball without falling over. And, when I was younger and forced into playing as part of the school curriculum, the coach would shout at me whenever I did something stupid and say things like, 'How can someone like Jason Waver have a brother as useless as you? You play like a girl,

Sam – why don't you go home and give your Barbie dolls a tea party?' Which was a bit ironic since, according to my brother Jason, if I played like a girl, if I played like *him*, then I would have been really good.

When the coach sat down in our living room in his tracksuit, I could see Mum looking at his trainers and wondering whether he was going to leave a mess on the carpet. Dad offered him a cup of tea and he said no, but if there was a beer going he'd have one of those.

'I'm sorry to turn up unannounced,' he said, after he'd finished half the bottle in one go, 'but there's a rumour going around the school at the moment. A rumour about Jason, I mean. And I thought we should have a talk.'

'What sort of rumour?' asked Mum, who'd come home much earlier than usual that day and was in a foul mood because the Prime Minister had given an interview in which he'd said he felt like a man half his age and had so much energy that he thought he could carry on for a long time yet.

'Just . . . a rumour,' said Coach O'Brien. 'But, if it's true, then something needs to be done about it. Of course, I know it's pointless to pay attention to gossip but –'

'I'm a politician, Mr O'Brien,' said Mum with a patient smile. 'I deal with rumours all day long. Why don't you just tell us what you've heard and then we can deal with it?'

'I'm sure it's nonsense,' he said, glancing towards my brother Jason, who was sitting with his hair tied back in a ponytail as usual and wearing a new shirt that looked as if it had been bought in Topshop rather than Topman. 'The thing is, you know I've always been a great fan of Jason's. He's the best footballer we have. The best we've had for years, if you ask me. And because of that, he's always been one of the most popular boys in school.'

'I'm sorry,' said Mum, interrupting him. 'You're saying he's popular *because* he's a good footballer or he's popular and, by chance, he also happens to be a good footballer?'

Coach O'Brien looked baffled. 'I'm sorry,' he said. 'I don't quite see the difference.'

'It doesn't matter,' she said. 'Please, go on.'

'The thing is,' he continued, 'I'm worried that something has happened between Jason and some of the other boys on the team. An argument of some sort. You know what schools are like – rumours get spread around all the time and most of them are complete rubbish. But we need to nip this one in the bud.'

No one said anything for a few moments, and I looked

towards Mum and Dad, who were staring down at the floor with expressions on their faces that I didn't quite recognize. It was almost as if they were offended on my brother Jason's behalf.

'Can you clarify what you've heard exactly?' asked Dad eventually. 'Just so we know exactly what we're dealing with here.'

'Perhaps you might like Sam to leave the room,' said the coach, nodding in my direction. 'He's a little young for –'

'Oh, I wouldn't worry about him,' said Mum. 'I learned long ago that there's no point trying to leave him out of things. He'll only listen at the door anyway. You might as well just spit it out, whatever it is.'

'Well,' he said, unable to look directly at any of us, and I could tell that whatever he was about to say was going to take a lot of resolve on his part, 'some of the boys are saying that Jason is . . . you know . . .'

'I'm what?' asked my brother Jason.

'A cannibal?' asked Dad. 'A vampire? French?'

'That he's going to quit the team,' said Coach O'Brien, swallowing nervously. 'That he doesn't want to play football any more.'

'Oh,' said Mum and Dad in unison. This obviously wasn't what they were expecting him to say.

'I haven't said that I don't want to play football any more,' said my brother Jason.

'I knew it,' said Coach O'Brien, sitting back and breathing a sigh of total relief. I don't think I'd ever seen anyone look so pleased before. 'I told people, no one who can take a free kick like Jason Waver would ever quit something he's so good at. It just wouldn't make any sense.'

'And this is the rumour you wanted to talk to us about?' asked Dad, a note of scepticism in his voice.

'Well, yes,' said Coach O'Brien with a shrug. 'That team is very important to me. For Jason to leave –'

'I'm sorry,' said Mum. 'It just seems . . . well, that's the *only* thing you wanted to talk to us about?'

Coach O'Brien scratched his head and looked at each of us in turn. 'I think so,' he said slowly. 'Unless there was something you wanted to discuss with me?'

'Obviously young people talk,' said Mum. 'And I dare say they've been gossiping about Jason's . . . situation.'

'What situation?' asked Coach O'Brien, looking completely baffled.

'That fact that I've told people I'm transgender, of course,' said my brother Jason. 'You're not pretending you haven't heard anything about that?'

'I've heard about it, yes,' said the coach with a shrug. 'But I don't see what that has to do with football . . .'

'So you're not here to say that you don't want him playing, then?' asked Mum, looking at him in astonishment.

'Why on earth would I not want him to play?' he asked.

'And the other boys on the team? They're not objecting? Or the parents?'

'Oh, a few are,' he admitted. 'Some of the boys have said some things. And I've had some letters from parents. But I've told them all the same thing.'

'Which is what?'

'That I couldn't care less if Jason wants to dress like Papa Smurf or to live his life like an alien from outer space. It's got nothing to do with me. But football! Football, now! That's different. That's something really important! The rest of it, well, who cares? It's not hurting anyone.'

I looked across at my brother Jason and we caught each other's eye. We shared the same look of disbelief and we couldn't help it: we just started laughing.

'I don't see what's so funny,' said Coach O'Brien, looking from one of us to the other. 'Also, my throat has gone very dry,' he added, and Dad took the hint, stood up and went to the kitchen to bring back two more bottles, handing one to the coach and keeping the other for himself.

'Let's be very clear here,' said Mum, smiling in the way she did whenever she answered questions from the other side in the House of Commons. At those moments she always spoke as if her opposite number was a complete simpleton and she wouldn't even bother to entertain her questions if she wasn't constitutionally obliged to. 'You're not here to make any complaints or to say that Jason can't play for the team any more. In fact, you're encouraging him to keep playing.'

'That's right,' said Coach O'Brien.

'You said that a few of the guys had objected,' said my brother Jason. 'And that you'd received some letters from parents. Who, exactly?'

'I don't think it matters who,' he replied.

'It matters to me. I've played with those guys for years. Since I was about six years old in some cases. I'd like to know who's so upset.'

The coach shrugged, then rattled off the names of a few boys. They were all familiar to me. Most of them were bullies who'd generally left me alone because of who my brother was, but I knew how they treated some of the younger boys and it wasn't nice.

'But they're my friends,' said my brother Jason, his voice a little quieter now as he sat back in the chair.

'But maybe . . .' said Mum, and I could see that she was choosing her words very carefully now. 'Should you maybe be thinking about how you're making the other players feel uncomfortable?' she asked. 'As you've said, Jason, these are your friends we're talking about here. You've known them all your life.'

'I can't control how anyone else feels,' he replied quietly.

'But if the parents are writing letters to Coach O'Brien, then maybe they might start writing letters to the papers too? And imagine how hurtful that would be to you,' she said. 'Perhaps there's an opportunity here, in fact. If we were to leave this issue alone for another year perhaps, just until you've finished school. Make sure that as few people find out as possible. And, in the meantime, you could leave the team and tell people that you've decided to drop out of extracurricular activities in order to focus on your studies.'

'But he can't leave the team!' cried Coach O'Brien. 'He's the best player we have! Or she! Whatever the right pronoun is!'

I stared at him in disbelief. I'd never yet heard anyone refer to my brother Jason as a *she*, and for it to be the football coach who did so astonished me.

'No, I think it's for the best,' said Mum, standing up and indicating to the coach that it was time for him to leave. 'And thank you for being so understanding. I promise, this whole thing will be sorted out as soon as possible. We have a wonderful psychologist working with Jason and hopefully things will go back to normal soon.'

'But the team!' said Coach O'Brien.

'Is not our concern.'

'No, but Jason is,' he replied. 'Do you want to stop playing?' he asked, looking across the room.

I expected him to say no, but I could see that he had been upset by the lack of support from the other players, although he, like me, was probably surprised by how understanding the coach was proving to be.

'Well, let's just take it day by day,' said Coach O'Brien in a not-very-convincing voice. 'And we'll see what happens.'

He shook hands with both my parents, ignored me entirely and then moved in the direction of my brother Jason before throwing his arms around him to wrap him in a bear hug. Perhaps I'd have to like him now, after all. It was very confusing. Yet another thing to be confused about, in fact.

After he left, my parents came back into the living room with furious expressions on their faces.

'Now look what's happened,' said Mum. 'It's only a matter of time until the papers get hold of it. How could you do this to me, Jason?' she cried. 'You're the most *selfish*, the most *irresponsible* –'

'I didn't do anything,' he said, bending over in the chair and starting to cry, loud gulping sounds that made me want to rush over and put my arms around him, but I couldn't. I felt like my feet had been superglued to the carpet. 'Please stop shouting at me!'

'I will not stop shouting at you until you put an end to this nonsense,' said Mum. 'You're going to ruin my career and your own life if you're not careful, but you don't care about that, do you? Oh no! You're not giving that a second thought. And for God's sake will you cut your hair! You look ridiculous!'

When my brother Jason eventually agreed to my parents' request that he stop playing football, I asked him whether he'd miss being part of the team and he shook his head and said that he'd never cared that much about it anyway, which I knew wasn't true. That was when he started to spend a lot of time alone in his room and, if I knocked, he'd tell me to go away. In the past, he'd always let me lie on his bed while he played music, or maybe he'd stretch out there with a book while I did my homework at his desk. He stopped helping me with my reading too, which upset me, as I always felt more confident when he was there to guide me. He had patience and didn't make me feel stupid when the words moved around the page rather than staying still. But now, when I asked for his help, he told me that I needed to figure it out for myself because the day would come when he wouldn't be living at home any more, he'd be at university or working in a job.

As our rooms were next to each other, sometimes I heard him crying when he went to bed, but when that happened I didn't want to go in anyway. His tears frightened me. I wanted my big brother to be strong. That was the way he'd always been and I didn't want him to change.

Soon after Coach O'Brien's visit, I walked into class one morning and the chatter in the room stopped immediately as every head turned in my direction. I could hear laughing and sniggering as usual when I sat down, but swore to myself that I wouldn't look up or acknowledge any of it.

'How's your sister, Sam?' asked my nemesis, David Fugue, turning round in his seat and grinning as he chewed the lid of his pen. 'Does she have a boyfriend yet? Although, don't look at me, I prefer a real woman.'

I ignored him and got my books out, praying that Mr Lowry would arrive quickly. It seemed like every day they had more and more jokes and, as the weeks wore on, they were starting to get to me.

'Hey, Sam,' said Liam Williamson, who sat in the chair behind me and was a disciple of David Fugue's. They went everywhere together, and he'd even got his hair cut just like David's, which made him look stupid. 'Did I hear that your sister's setting up a new girl band? They should go on *The X-Factor*!'

'Shut up, Williamson,' I said.

'Make me.'

'I will if you don't shut up.'

'I'm still talking.'

'Then you better stop.'

'What will you do if I don't?'

'I'll make you.'

'Go on, then.'

'Just wait and see.'

'That's what I'm doing. But I'm not seeing anything.'

'I've got three brothers,' shouted James Burke from the other side of the room, tossing a crumpled-up piece of paper in my direction so it bounced off my head and landed, pretty amazingly, in the wastepaper basket. 'You can have one of them if you like. It can't be easy just having a sister. Or do you both sit around in the evening and talk about boys you like while plaiting each other's hair?'

That was it. I'd had enough. I leaped out of my seat and ran towards him, and we threw ourselves on top of each other, to the great delight of our classmates, who gathered around in a circle, cheering us on as we started to fight. It only lasted a minute, though, because Mr Lowry came in and the rest of the class scattered as he shouted at us to sit down. I was still lying on the floor, however, slightly dazed, and I could feel something running down my chin. When I pressed a finger to my mouth, it came back red and, as my tongue moved across my lower lip, I tasted the bittersweet flavour of blood from where James had punched me.

'What's going on here?' asked Mr Lowry. 'Sam, what happened to you?'

'Nothing, sir,' I said, standing up but unwilling to look him in the eye.

'It's obviously not nothing. You've been fighting. Who started this?'

No one said anything but there was a lot of muffled giggling.

'You're like a bunch of children,' he said angrily.

'We're thirteen, sir,' said Liam Williamson. 'We *are* children.'

'Don't get smart with me.'

'But it's school. Isn't that why I'm here?'

Mr Lowry rolled his eyes and looked like he was doing his best to control his temper. 'You know, some day, when you're all older,' he said, looking around the room, 'you're going to have troubles of your own and you'll have friends who are going through tough times. Maybe it'll even be one of your own children. And when that happens, you'll look back at the way you're all behaving now and wonder whether you might not have been able to show a little more kindness.'

The room was silent. Even David Fugue had nothing to say to that.

'Go down to the office, Sam,' he said finally with a sigh, knowing there was no point trying to have a sensible conversation with a group of kids too frightened of risking their own reputations to behave with any compassion. 'They'll sort you out.'

'I'm fine,' I said, wanting to go back to my seat so I wouldn't appear weak in front of the others.

'You're not fine, you're bleeding. Away with you and don't come back until you're all cleaned up.'

I snorted angrily and marched out of the room to the sound of jeers behind me before making my way down the corridor to the office. Mrs Wilson took one look at me and gave her usual speech about how she wished she worked in an all-girls' school where she might at least be surrounded by young ladies instead of total thugs, and I thought about telling her that, in my experience, girls were even worse than boys when it came to bullying but decided against it. When she finished scolding me, she took an ice pack from the freezer and instructed me to hold it against my lower lip for a few minutes.

'It won't need stitches,' she said. 'But you know that I'll have to report you to the head for fighting, right?'

'I don't care.'

'And you'll probably get a detention.'

'Big deal.'

'You're a very rude boy, do you know that? Did your parents not teach you any manners?'

'No. They're even worse than I am.'

'Well!' she said, looking outraged. 'The apple doesn't fall far from the tree, that's for sure. I've seen your mother on *Question Time* and she speaks to the audience like they're a room full of idiots. I can see where you get your charm from. How do your teeth feel anyway?' she asked. 'Is anything loose in there?'

I ran my tongue around the inside of my mouth, but everything seemed intact. 'They're fine,' I mumbled from behind the ice pack.

'You boys and your fighting,' she said. 'And it's always over the most insignificant things. What was this one about anyway? Probably something of – Oh!'

She stopped and put a hand to her mouth, then closed her eyes as if she'd suddenly remembered something.

'Of course. You're Jason's brother.'

'Yes,' I said.

'That explains it,' she said, her tone softening. 'Well, then, it seems to me that you must be very different from him to carry on this way.'

'Why?' I asked, frowning.

'Because fighting is a pretty cowardly thing to do. Trying to win whatever argument you're having simply by hurting someone else. And, if you ask me, Jason is the bravest boy in this entire school.'

I didn't make any reply to this, even though her words had surprised me, and thirty minutes later I was on my way back to class. The corridors were empty and, as I had no desire to see any of my so-called friends, I sat down on a bench, feeling sick inside, and looked up at the clock on the wall. It was still only first period – there was an entire day to get through, and I didn't think I'd manage. I glanced to my left when I heard footsteps approaching and, to my surprise, I saw my brother Jason walking towards me.

'What are you doing out here?' he asked.

'Nothing.'

'What happened to your face?'

I shrugged. 'I was in a fight,' I said.

'With who?'

'What does it matter?'

'With who, Sam?'

I said nothing, looking up at him with a mixture of accusation and wounded pride. He was still wearing that stupid ponytail and make-up, and when he sat down next to me I moved up a little because I felt so angry. I wanted to walk away, but I knew that if I did he'd follow me and try to talk it over, and the last thing I wanted was to discuss any of this with him.

'Was it because of me?' he asked. 'Is that why you were fighting?'

'What are you even doing here?' I asked, raising my voice. 'Why aren't you in class? This is the junior corridor – you're not supposed to be down here.'

'I was using the bathroom. The upstairs disabled one is being painted so I had to use the one on this floor.'

'There's a *boys'* on that floor.'

'I don't use the boys' any more, you know that. And I'm not allowed to use the girls'.'

'Just go back upstairs,' I said, pushing him away.

'I'm not leaving you when you're this upset.'

'I'm not upset!' I insisted.

'Yes you are. It's obvious that you are. Are you angry with me?'

'No.'

'You won't even look at me.'

'I don't *want* to look at you.'

'Talk to me, Sam.'

'*Now* you want to talk,' I said, turning to him furiously as I felt the tears building behind my eyes. 'When we're at home you sit in your room all the time and won't even let me in. What are you even doing in there anyway – trying on dresses?'

He bit his lip and looked away before shaking his head. 'No,' he said. 'No, I'm not trying on dresses.'

'Make-up then? Putting on lipstick and mascara to make yourself look like a girl?'

He said nothing for a long time, but I could hear him breathing steadily next to me as one foot tapped on the floor.

'I suppose I didn't think all this through before I told

you and Mum and Dad,' he said eventually. 'I didn't realize how badly it would affect you.'

'No. You didn't.'

'I just felt that if I didn't tell someone I was going to go mad. Or worse.'

'Worse?' I asked, turning to him. 'What could be worse than what's happening right now?'

'I just thought that, if I told people, then things would get easier,' he said.

'And have they?' I asked. 'Because they don't seem any easier to me.'

'No,' he said. 'Probably not. But I don't regret it. Because at least I'm being honest with myself at last. Tell me the truth. You got hit because of me, didn't you?'

I nodded.

'Did you hit whoever it was back?'

'Of course I did.'

'You don't have to stand up for me, you know. Let them say whatever they want to say. Who cares? It's just words.'

'I care,' I said.

'Well, I don't.'

'You're not in my class. You don't have to listen to them.'

'No, but I'm in *my* class, and do you think that's any

easier? All these years I've been the most popular boy in school. Captain of the football team. And now they're all calling me names and scrawling things on my locker. Lots of people I thought of as friends have deserted me. If you think that's easy –'

'But you started it!' I cried, jumping up in frustration. 'It's all your fault!'

'I know,' he said. 'But what else could I do? Tell me. What would you have done if it was you?'

'But it wouldn't have been me,' I insisted. 'Because I'm a boy. I've always been a boy and I always *will* be a boy, and nothing will ever change that.'

'Well, then, you're lucky, aren't you?' he said. 'You don't have any confusion about yourself. You're not being torn apart inside. But I am. And –'

Before he could finish, the bell rang and the doors of the classrooms started to open. I panicked, not wanting anyone to see me with him, and took advantage of the rush of bodies to make my escape.

I stayed awake that night on purpose, and whenever I felt as if I was dropping off to sleep I jumped up with a start and slapped my hands back and forth across my face before climbing out of bed and marching around the room like a soldier on sentry duty. Every so often I'd check the time, but the clock seemed to be moving slower than ever. I thought about going downstairs and watching television on the quietest volume possible, but Mum and Dad's room was right over the living room and I guessed that I'd wake them up. My plan was to wait until two o'clock in the morning, because I'd read on the internet that this was the time when most people were at the deepest point of their sleep cycle and were least likely to wake up if disturbed.

Eventually the time came and I opened my bedside drawer. Earlier in the evening I'd snuck something in there that I'd brought up from the kitchen and, as I held it in my hands, it felt both heavy and dangerous. I made my way towards my bedroom door and opened it very slowly to ensure that it wouldn't creak, stopping only briefly on the landing to check that I hadn't disturbed anyone and that the house was completely at peace. After a few moments I crept barefoot towards my brother Jason's room and carefully turned the handle, letting the door open only a few millimetres at a time.

His curtains weren't quite pulled together at the centre, and as the moonlight slipped in I could see him breathing heavily in his sleep, his mouth a little open, the sheets pulled halfway down his chest. He shifted in the bed and made a slight grunting sound, and as he turned his head I saw that he hadn't taken the scrunchie out of his hair and the ponytail that everyone hated was lying flat against the pillow.

I stepped towards him and very gently lifted it. Then I took the scissors I was carrying, opened them between my thumb and index finger, and slowly let them close across his hair. The scissors were sharp and did the job quickly, cutting through with a deeply satisfying slicing sound. A moment later I found myself standing in the middle of his bedroom, holding the ponytail in my hand. He shuffled a little more in his sleep before rolling over again, and then, with a deep sigh, settled back into his dream as I made my way back to my room, closing the door quietly behind me and opening my special box with the lock and key at the back of my wardrobe, putting the ponytail on top of Mum's old copies of *Vogue* and locking it again before hiding the key.

When I climbed back into bed I lay there for a long time, my heart pounding in my chest, uncertain whether I had done the right thing or not. At least now Mum and Dad would stop shouting at him to get a haircut. Perhaps, I reasoned, when he woke up and saw himself in the mirror he would remember that he was a boy and put all this rubbish behind him. I was doing him a favour, I told myself as I rolled over and closed my eyes. Soon, everyone in his class would stop making fun of him.

And of me.

I could go back to being invisible.

6

The Brewsters

Over the weeks that followed, my brother Jason stopped talking to either Mum or Dad and barely spoke to me. He ate all his meals in his bedroom with the door shut, and one afternoon, when I came home from school, I found him installing a bolt on his bedroom door.

'No one's getting in here without my say-so from now on,' he said when he saw me standing at the top of the staircase, watching him. 'Coming into my room like that when I was asleep was the most cowardly thing either of them could have done.'

'But they both say they didn't do it,' I told him, for Mum and Dad had each insisted that they were innocent of cutting off his ponytail, although they both made it clear that they were glad it was finally gone. No one even thought to blame me.

'Well, it didn't just fall off of its own accord, did it?' he asked. 'There.' He stood back and admired his handiwork, sliding the bolt back and forth a few times to make sure that it worked. 'Anyway, the joke's on them, because I'm just going to grow it back. My hair grows so quickly anyway. I'll have it again by spring.'

The atmosphere in our house during those weeks was very strained, and it only grew worse when, two days before Christmas, my brother Jason came downstairs carrying a holdall and announced that he was going away for a week and wouldn't be back until the new year.

'What?' asked Mum, looking up from her iPad. 'What are you talking about? Tomorrow's Christmas Eve!'

'I don't intend to stay here for Christmas,' he said, looking her directly in the eye. 'I can't just sit around eating turkey and pretending that we're a happy family when that just isn't the case.'

'I don't see why not,' said Dad. 'That's what everyone else does at Christmas.'

'Well, I don't like being a hypocrite, that's all.'

'Look,' continued Dad, standing up and putting a hand on my brother Jason's shoulder for a moment before taking it away again. 'We don't have to talk about your . . . situation, if that's what you're worried about.'

'That sounds really healthy,' replied my brother Jason. 'And it makes me feel really good about myself. Anything else you'd like to just brush under the carpet and ignore while we're at it?'

'No, I don't think so,' he said, considering it. 'Deborah, have you got anything?'

'Nothing springs to mind,' said Mum.

'Good. Because Christmas is a time for family,' said Dad. 'For people who love each other to be together.'

'But you don't love me,' said my brother Jason, raising his voice now. 'If you loved me, then you wouldn't have crept into my room when I was asleep and cut my hair off!'

'Oh, for the hundredth time,' said Mum in an exasperated tone. 'We didn't –'

'Do you want to know the truth, Jason?' asked Dad.

'If you're willing to tell me it, yes.'

'You might not like what you hear.'

'Well, I didn't much like being the victim of an unprovoked assault either, so go ahead.'

'Oh, for pity's sake,' said Mum, shaking her head.

'I know exactly who cut that stupid ponytail off,' continued Dad. 'And it wasn't your mum or me.'

'Go on, then,' said my brother Jason. 'Who was it?'

Dad glanced over at me and I felt my blood turn cold. Had he guessed the truth?

'You're sure you want to know?' he asked.

'I'm completely sure.'

'All right, then,' said Dad with a shrug. 'The fact is – and I can't believe you haven't figured this out by now – you cut it off yourself.'

My brother Jason stared at him for a few moments before shaking his head and starting to laugh. 'Is that supposed to be some sort of joke?' he asked.

'No. It might sound ridiculous but just hear me out. You woke up in the middle of the night, looked into the mirror and your subconscious told you that you were pretending to be someone you're not. And so you cut off your ponytail, then went back to sleep and remembered nothing about it the next day. It's obvious. You've blocked out the memory because it contradicts the things you're saying aloud.'

'That's a really interesting hypothesis,' said Mum, nodding her head.

'It makes perfect sense when you think about it,' said Dad.

'It doesn't make any sense whatsoever,' said my brother Jason.

'The subconscious can be a very powerful thing. You

should talk to Dr Watson about it the next time you see him. I bet he'd agree with us.'

'Well, he hasn't agreed with you on anything so far,' he said, for he'd been seeing Dr Watson once a fortnight since all this began, but after our first visit he'd always gone alone. 'So it seems doubtful. Anyway, I'm not spending Christmas here this year and there's nothing you can do about it. I've packed a bag and I'm going. You can't stop me.'

'But what about your toys?' asked Dad. 'They're already wrapped and under the tree.'

'I'm seventeen,' he said, throwing his hands in the air. 'I don't want toys.'

'I meant your presents. It's just a figure of speech.'

'I don't want anything from you,' he said. 'At least, nothing that you can wrap up and put under a Christmas tree.'

'More to the point, where will you go?' asked Dad. 'It's not as if you can afford a hotel.'

'I'm going to Aunt Rose's,' he said.

'Oh no,' said Mum, leaping up from her chair, for this, of course, was the final straw as far as she was concerned. 'You can't be serious.'

'I'm completely serious.'

'You're telling me that you would rather spend

Christmas, the most important time of the year, with your Aunt Rose than with your own family?'

'She *is* part of our family,' said my brother Jason. 'Even though we pretend that she isn't.'

Aunt Rose was my mother's sister, younger by two years, but they had never seen eye to eye, and for that reason she didn't come to visit very often, even though she only lived about fifty miles away, in the house she and Mum had grown up in, having bought Mum out of her half after my grandparents' death. But she was the opposite of Mum in every possible way.

TEN THINGS THAT AUNT ROSE HAD DONE THAT
MUM NEVER HAD OR WOULD

1. She'd jumped out of a plane and parachuted to the ground.
2. She'd been married to three different men and divorced them all.
3. She'd spent four weeks in jail for punching a policeman at a 'Stop the War' march in 2003.
4. She'd lived in something called a commune when she was nineteen. Then she lived in something called a kibbutz. Then she lived in Milton Keynes.
5. She'd appeared as an extra in a *Star Wars* movie.

6. She'd thrown an egg at Prince Charles and it broke on his shoulder.
7. She'd written a book of poetry and published it with a really important publishing house called the Rose Press.
8. She'd climbed the Sydney Harbour Bridge.
9. She had a tattoo of someone called David Bowie on her arm.
10. She'd told my brother Jason that he could come to stay with her for Christmas and be whoever he wanted to be while he was there.

'It's out of the question,' said Mum. 'That woman will just encourage you in your delusions. My God, she'll probably strap you down and cut it off.'

'Cut what off?' I asked.

'It's you who cuts things off, remember,' said my brother Jason angrily.

'We didn't touch your blasted ponytail,' shouted Mum. 'Although I'm glad it's gone if you want to know the truth. At least now you look like a real boy.'

'I'm not Pinocchio,' roared my brother Jason, although he didn't say it quite like that. And he included another word before 'Pinocchio'. One that rhymes with 'ducking'.

'No, it's not a good idea. I don't want Rose involved in any of this.'

'Well, she already is,' said my brother Jason after a long pause.

'What?' asked Mum, looking across at him.

'I said she already is.'

I glanced at Mum, who swallowed noticeably. She had a wounded expression on her face that was hard to look at.

'You've already told her what's going on?'

'Yes.'

'How much have you told her?'

'Everything. I call her almost every day.'

'Of course you do,' said Mum, looking down at her lap now. Her voice had gone very quiet.

'Deborah,' said Dad, but she shook her head and cut him off.

'It's fine,' she said.

'It's not fine!'

'It is. If he thinks he can talk to her instead of me, his own mother, then –'

'I've *tried* to talk to you!' shouted my brother Jason. 'But you don't listen! Aunt Rose listens to me! And she doesn't treat me like I've got some sort of disease!'

'You're breaking my heart,' said Mum.

'I don't want to hurt you,' said my brother Jason, his tone softening a little. 'I'm just trying to be honest with myself, that's all. You're not helping me right now, that's the truth of it. Maybe you're trying, I don't know, but it's not working. So, I'm leaving now, and I'll be at Aunt Rose's if you need me.'

'But when will you be back?' I asked, standing up, feeling very upset at the idea of a Christmas Day without him. If it was because of the ponytail after all, then it was my fault. But I couldn't bring myself to admit it to him.

'I'm not sure. By New Year probably.'

'Can I go with you?'

'No, you can't, Sam,' snapped Dad, who was sitting down again and looking miserable.

'But I don't want to spend Christmas without him!' I shouted.

'None of us does. But it seems like he's made up his mind. And we might not be able to tell *him* what to do, but we can certainly tell *you*.'

'I've left a present on your bed,' said my brother Jason quietly, coming over and trying to give me a hug, but I pulled away. Instead, I just sat down on the sofa with my head in my hands, wishing all this was just a bad dream and that I'd wake up soon.

'Well, if you're going, then go!' shouted Mum eventually. 'There's no point just standing there, staring at us!'

And, with that, my brother Jason shrugged his shoulders, picked up his holdall and left. The rest of us sat in silence until, finally, Mum leaped from her chair and ran out on to the street, looking left and right.

'Jason!' she shouted. 'Jason!'

But it was too late. He'd already gone.

It was the worst Christmas of my life. Perhaps knowing that the atmosphere would be strained with just three of us around the dinner table, Mum invited one of her colleagues from the parliamentary party over with his wife and their fourteen-year-old daughter, Laura, who seemed furious at having to spend Christmas Day in someone else's house, but I could tell from the moment they arrived that Mum's colleague – Mr Brewster, although he told me to call him Bobby – was thrilled to be there and determined to do everything he could to impress. Bobby's wife, Stephanie, was also sucking up like crazy.

'It's so good of you to do this, Secretary of State,' said Bobby when we eventually sat down to dinner. Turkey, ham, three types of potato, chipolata sausages, four different vegetables and lashings of gravy. The kind of meal that, under different circumstances, I would have loved.

'Oh, please, no formality today,' said Mum. 'Call me Deborah.'

'Deborah, then. You're very kind. After the year we've had, a little generosity of spirit is such a nice thing.'

'Yes, it's been an awful few months,' said Stephanie.

'Why? What happened?' I asked, momentarily interested.

'Our travel company went bust,' said Bobby. 'So we lost a deposit we'd put down on a holiday in the Seychelles.'

'And the waiting list was so long for the new BMW,' added Stephanie, 'that we ended up having to settle for last year's model.'

'Please,' said Bobby. 'Don't mention models.'

'Sore subject?' asked Dad.

'Dad!' said Laura, who was sitting uncomfortably close to me and who I could barely bring myself to look at. She had pale skin and bright blue eyes, and every time she turned in my direction I wanted to run away and hide behind the sofa, like a nervous puppy. She'd asked me my name earlier and it had taken me almost fifteen seconds to remember it.

'Oh, Deborah, listen to this story,' said Stephanie, putting her knife and fork down. 'You won't believe it. A couple of months ago, Laura and I were shopping in Oxford Street and we decided to go into Topshop. Of course, it's not somewhere I would go into myself usually, but Laura insisted. Well, we weren't in the door for more than a few minutes when a woman came over and introduced herself as a scout from the Better Than You Model Agency. She said that Laura had such a great look and that her walk ... well, it turns out that she'd been watching her walking around the store and she'd never seen anything like it!'

'So flattering,' said Laura, rolling her eyes. 'My great skill, it seems, is that I can put one foot in front of the other and achieve forward momentum. What should I dream of next?'

'Laura, please,' said Stephanie, placing a hand atop her daughter's for a moment. 'Mummy's talking, Laura's listening. Anyway,' she continued, turning back to Mum, 'the scout asked whether Laura might like to stop by their offices to have some photos taken and, naturally, I was beside myself. What an opportunity! But throughout the entire conversation, this so-called daughter of mine just stood there with a face on her like she'd swallowed a wasp.'

'Because I don't . . . want . . . to be . . . a model,' said Laura, between gritted teeth, and her pauses made me understand that she had said this at least a thousand times to her mother since that afternoon in Topshop.

'Well, anyway, to cut a long story short, I managed to persuade the ungrateful little so-and-so to come to the photo session even though it was like pulling teeth. Honestly, a chance that thousands of girls would give their left leg for!'

'They wouldn't be very good models if they only had one leg,' said Bobby, laughing with his mouth open so I could see all his Christmas dinner being mashed up together inside and it was totally gross. 'It wouldn't be a signature walk then so much as a signature hop!'

'That's rude,' I said quietly. 'Anyway, I've seen models on TV with only one leg.'

'No you haven't,' said Bobby.

'Yes I have.'

'No you haven't.'

'Yes I have.'

'Didn't Paul McCartney marry someone with only one leg?' asked Dad.

'Do be quiet, everyone,' said Mum. 'Sorry, Stephanie, please continue.'

'Yes, well, we went for the photos and, in fairness to

her, Laura did everything they asked of her. Posed the way they wanted her to pose, looked into the camera, away from the camera, held her hands in certain ways. I mean, I don't understand it all, obviously I'm not model material myself . . .' She paused for a few moments and looked around the table. I think she was waiting for someone to contradict her but, as no one did, not even her husband, she went back to her story. 'Anyway,' she said, 'when it was all over, a group of people from Better Than You gathered in front of a computer screen looking at the pictures and I could tell how excited they all were. And then another woman came over and introduced herself as the head of the agency and said that she'd like to make Laura an offer on the spot. *I think we can guarantee editorial*, she told us, *and couture. I haven't seen someone so natural since Kate, and that was, like, a hundred years ago. Your daughter is going to be famous*, she said.'

'But that's wonderful,' said Mum, who looked as if she was growing bored by the story now, particularly when she didn't have anything equally thrilling to share. 'Congratulations! You must be so excited!'

'How could I be,' asked Stephanie, 'when Laura, my oh-so-intelligent daughter, said no!'

'She said what?'

'I don't want to be a model,' repeated Laura. 'I don't know what part of that sentence confuses you. I've been very clear on this.'

'But that's ridiculous,' said Dad. 'Look at you, you're absolutely drop-dead gorgeous. My God, if I was thirty years younger, twenty even –'

Everyone turned to look at him and he blushed scarlet. 'For someone your age, I mean,' he said, coughing quickly and raising his handkerchief to his mouth. 'Obviously you're very young and –'

'But I don't understand,' said Mum, sounding completely baffled. 'An opportunity like this lands in your lap once in a lifetime, if at all. And you decide not to take advantage of it? What's wrong with you? Is there something else you want to do with your life?'

'I want to be a gardener,' said Laura.

'A what? I'm sorry, I thought you said a gardener.'

'I did say a gardener.'

Mum looked beyond confused now. 'As in someone who tidies gardens?' she asked eventually.

'A landscape gardener, I mean,' said Laura. She looked around at us and her expression changed from fed up to enthusiastic. 'I want to design gardens, big gardens, small gardens, formal, informal. Have you ever been to the Chelsea Flower Show, Mrs Waver?'

'Yes, of course,' said Mum. 'I go every year on the same day the Queen goes. It's a tremendous opportunity for someone in my position. Even though I get terrible hay fever. But that's the price one pays to climb the greasy pole!'

'I go every year too,' said Laura.

'You can blame me for that,' said Bobby. 'I took her there when she was only four or five years old and she's insisted on going back every year since.'

'And from that first time, I've known that's what I want to do.'

'I'm sorry,' said Mum. 'Are you saying that you'd rather spend your life up to your elbows in soil than on the catwalks of Rome, Milan and New York in the latest Oscar de la Renta dress? Is that actually what you're telling me?'

'Yes,' said Laura, popping a carrot into her mouth.

'Extraordinary,' said Mum, shaking her head. 'I simply do not understand the young people of today. We give them every opportunity they could wish for and they throw it back in our faces.'

'They're like monkeys in the zoo chucking their faeces around,' said Dad.

'Alan,' said Mum, closing her eyes briefly in distaste. 'No faeces at the dinner table, please.'

'Sorry, Deborah.'

'We can't have willies at the breakfast table either,' I whispered to Laura, and then, realizing what I'd just said, my face went from white to red in about three seconds too.

Laura snorted a little in laughter before shaking her head. 'I would be happy if I was a gardener,' she said. 'That's all I want.'

'It's just been an awful few months,' sighed Stephanie. 'But let's hope next year is better.'

'Yes indeed,' said Bobby, putting his knife and fork down and smiling widely as he lifted his glass of wine. 'Of course, who knows? Perhaps this time next year you won't be celebrating Christmas in this house at all?' he added.

'Oh, well,' said Mum, doing her best to look uncomfortable. 'Let's not get ahead of ourselves.'

'Why wouldn't we have Christmas here?' I asked. 'We're not moving, are we?'

'No, Sam,' said Dad. 'We're not. Not yet anyway. But who knows what the future holds?'

'Christmas at Number Ten,' said Bobby. 'Now that really would be something, wouldn't it?'

'But this *is* number ten,' I pointed out, for our house was, indeed, number ten on our street.

'There's no vacancy right now,' said Mum. 'And, that being the case, the Prime Minister has my full support. Should a vacancy appear in the future, however, one would of course need to consider one's position and seek the advice of colleagues.'

'I'm sorry,' said Bobby, laughing loudly and slapping the table with his hand. 'Has the man from Sky News just walked in? Faisal Islam, get out from under the table, there's a good fellow, and help yourself to some food!'

He looked around the room in high spirits but, perhaps seeing how Mum's expression had changed to one of disapproval, he stopped rather quickly. 'Well, you're quite right of course, Secretary of State,' he said. 'Secretary of Waver. I mean, Mrs Waver. Deborah. No point looking for a position that isn't even available. But of course, in the fullness of time, I hope you know that I think you would make an excellent –'

'Thank you, Bobby,' said Mum, smiling. 'That means a great deal to me. Particularly considering how many in the party would look to you for guidance. I suspect many of them would be cheered to see you in one of the high offices of state in the not-too-distant future.'

'Which one?' asked Stephanie, leaning forward.

'Again, we're getting ahead of ourselves,' said Mum.

'And it's Christmas Day. Let's just enjoy our meal and leave the politics behind us.'

I could sense a certain disappointment around the table that this part of the conversation had come to an end.

'But don't you have another son?' asked Stephanie eventually, after we'd endured about ten minutes of discussing the possibility of snow before New Year.

'Another son?' asked Mum, looking up and frowning as if she wasn't entirely sure.

'Yes, I thought you had two?'

'Oh, you mean Jason,' said Mum. 'Yes, he's seventeen now.'

'And he's not with you for Christmas?'

'No, he's volunteering,' she said.

'Volunteering?'

'Yes.'

'Where?'

'At a homeless shelter in the East End.'

Both Bobby and Stephanie put their knives and forks down and looked suitably impressed. Even Laura glanced up and raised an eyebrow as if she was interested at last.

'On Christmas Day?' asked Bobby.

'Well, naturally we would have preferred that he

spend the time with us,' said Dad. 'But the thing about Jason is that he has this extraordinary sense of public service and duty. He gets that from Deborah, of course. And he felt that, as he has access to so many privileges in life, this year he wanted to give something back.'

'You must be very proud,' said Stephanie. 'I wish I had a child like that instead of someone as ungrateful as Laura.'

'I'm ungrateful,' said Laura, turning to me as if I was some distant audience, 'simply because I don't want to be a model.'

'You could be a model,' I said quietly. 'You're really beautiful.'

Everyone turned to look at me and I wished that the ground would open up beneath me and swallow me whole.

'Well, I think you should be very proud,' said Bobby. 'A son like that, giving back on Christmas Day. The party would appreciate that. I hope you've let the press secretary know. We could still get a few snappers down there to take some pictures. Play very well with the backbenchers, that would.'

'Actually, Bobby,' said Mum, looking slightly nervous now, 'I think it's best if you don't mention this to anyone. Jason's choices are his own, of course, and I would hate anyone to think that I was using them for political gain.'

'Say no more,' said Bobby with a wink of his eye. 'Just a quiet word to someone from the *Daily* –'

'No, I mean it,' she said, raising her voice. 'I actually do mean it. I don't want anyone to find out about it. Let's just let him do this by himself. It's a private matter.'

'Well, if you're sure,' said Bobby, who looked uncertain whether she actually meant it or not.

'I'm completely sure,' she replied. 'In fact, I think it would be best if we leave my family entirely out of any future campaign. I'd prefer to focus solely on policies.'

Although I went upstairs after dinner to try to read a book, I ran into Laura again just before the Brewsters went home. She was coming out of the bathroom and I was stepping out on to the landing when she cornered me.

'Can I see your room?' she asked me, and I froze. A girl had never set foot in my room before. Only Mum, and she didn't count. My brother Jason's ex-girlfriend Penny had tried to come in once, but I'd put a chair against the door and refused to come out until she went home.

'Why?' I asked.

'Because they're talking politics downstairs again and I want to bang my head against the table until I pass out. Come on, don't make me go back down there.'

I hesitated, but there didn't seem to be anything I could do to get out of it, so we went inside. I glanced around quickly for anything incriminating. There were two pairs of boxer shorts on the floor and I kicked them under the bed but, other than that, everything seemed to be in order. Not even an old issue of *Vogue* on display. She threw herself on the bed and stretched out, and I moved as far away from her as possible, sitting with my back to the wall and wrapping my arms around my knees.

'Do you know Lisa Turnbull?' she asked me, and I nodded, for Lisa was in my class at school and was almost as horrible to me as my nemesis, David Fugue. Whenever I got a new spot she'd point it out to everyone.

'Yes,' I said.

'Do you like her?'

I hesitated, unsure whether or not I should be honest. 'How do you know her?' I asked.

'I don't, really. I know her older sister, who's a monster. We used to be friends, but we aren't any more.'

'Why not?'

'Because she's a gossip. And she's never happier than when she's causing chaos in other people's lives.'

'Right,' I said.

'Do you have a girlfriend?' she asked then, and I could feel my stomach start to twist and turn in strange ways.

'No one special,' I said.

'What does that mean?'

'No, I don't have a girlfriend.'

'OK.'

She jumped off the bed then and went over to my bookcase and started looking through the books, pulling a few out and glancing at the covers.

'Are these really yours?' she asked, frowning.

'Yes,' I said. 'Why?'

'They're for young kids. Don't you read anything for our age group?'

'I'm dyslexic,' I told her. 'I'm not very good with books but I like to read, so I end up reading books for young kids a lot of the time. Just to help me get through them better. Except for Sherlock Holmes stories. They're not for kids but I really try with them because they're so good.'

'Oh right,' she said, putting the books back. 'Sorry, I didn't mean to be rude.'

'That's OK, you weren't.'

'If it's any consolation, I couldn't tie my shoelaces until I was ten. And I still can't whistle.'

'That's crazy,' I said, laughing.

'I know. I don't have very good hand-to-eye coordination. So, tell me the truth,' she said then. 'Your brother isn't really helping out at a homeless shelter, is he?'

'Yes he is,' I said. 'Why would you say that?'

'Because when your mother said so you looked up like you were in total shock.'

'I just didn't know that she was going to tell anyone, that's all.'

'I saw a photograph of him in your living room,' she said. 'He's cute.'

'He's seventeen,' I said. 'And you're only fourteen.'

'I know. I'm just saying. Anyway, you look quite like him.'

I frowned, unsure what to say to this.

'Relax, Sam,' she said. 'It's a compliment.'

And then she smiled at me and went back downstairs, and I stayed in my room and it smelled like her perfume. And, for the first time in a long time, I didn't think about my brother Jason at all for the rest of the night.

7

Aunt Rose's House

By mid-January, my brother Jason still hadn't come home and, although I missed him, I also found that life had become a lot less complicated with him not around. I talked to him on the phone sometimes but found that we didn't have a lot to say to each other. The school had given him permission to be home-schooled, by Aunt Rose, for a few weeks while he dealt with what they called his 'personal issues'.

When classes started back, I'd become invisible again because the other students had moved on to new sources of scandal, such as the fact that our geography teacher had left his wife, who was also our maths teacher, for a different woman and, as she happened to be our science teacher, all three were often to be seen having arguments in the corridors between classes. Also, our headmaster had bought a Harley-Davidson motorbike and was driving it in every morning wearing full leathers, which delighted, appalled and embarrassed us all at the same time.

TEN THINGS THAT NO ONE OVER THIRTY-FIVE SHOULD EVER DO

1. Buy a Harley-Davidson motorbike and drive it to school every morning wearing full leathers.
2. Use the words 'dude', 'bro', 'brah', 'sup' or 'lol'.
3. Dance.
4. Tell their class that they have a 'killer hangover' and everyone needs to keep their voice down. It doesn't impress us. Not even a little bit.
5. Talk about their collection of *Star Wars* figurines.
6. Pretend not to watch *Countdown*. We know you do, that you think you're really good at the numbers game and that you'd do anything to appear on it.
7. Wear Converse runners or dress shoes without socks.
8. Talk about bands from centuries ago like Oasis.
9. Begin a sentence with the words 'In my day'.
10. Have sex. That's just gross.

My nemesis, David Fugue, continued to torment me, but it was no longer about my brother Jason. To be fair, I gave him quite a few targets. I had spots on my forehead and, because his skin was so *perfect*, he called me names and threw bottles of Clearasil at me. And when I found a few moustache hairs growing on my upper lip I used a Sharpie to make them look darker and more noticeable, but they just ended up looking like I'd drawn them on and it's almost impossible to wash Sharpie off – it lasts for *days*. And then he found me writing the name Laura on the front of a notebook with love hearts around it – I hadn't even realized that I was doing it – and told everyone that I'd fallen in love with a girl, so I was the gayest guy in school, which didn't really make a lot of sense, but people went along with it anyway. Except for Jake Tomlin, that is, who *is* gay and told everyone last year. Jake said I wasn't gay, that he knew his snails from his oysters – whatever that meant – and I wanted to thank him but wasn't sure whether he'd be offended by that so I left it alone.

At home, no one mentioned the fact that there was one person missing from our lives, and it felt at times as if my brother Jason had been forgotten by everyone except me. Mum and Dad barely noticed my presence and were constantly glued to their phones, iPads and laptops. Almost every night there were people from the party in our house, so it was almost impossible for me to watch TV, and they kept running down lists of names, trying to decide whether each person they mentioned was a Definite Yes, a Definite No or a Persuadable. When I asked Mum what she was trying to persuade them to do, she said 'to put their trust in me'.

So it probably shouldn't come as too much of a surprise that, when I vanished from home in the spring half-term, it was hours before anyone even realized that I was gone.

It started when I received an unexpected letter. I never received letters, only the occasional birthday card, so it came as something of a shock to find one waiting on the kitchen table for me one morning. When I opened it, there was a twenty-pound note inside as well as a brief letter:

Dear Sam,

Come and stay for a few nights! Here's some money for a ticket. I'll pick you up at five o'clock on Friday at Oxford station.

Peace,
Aunt Rose

AN ELEVENTH THING THAT NO ONE OVER
THIRTY-FIVE SHOULD EVER DO

11. Say 'Peace'.

I was happy to receive the letter – and the money – but not at all surprised that she'd suddenly asked me to stay. She had a history of doing random things like that, after all. Once, she'd invited a homeless man to move in for a few days so he could get over a cold, and he ended up becoming my Uncle Bernie for two years until she divorced him. Another time, she took in a family of Syrian refugees and they lived with her for six months, and Mum said we couldn't visit as it might not play well with the backbenchers if it got out. And when Prince Philip retired, she even invited him to come and stay with her, saying they could take walks together and make blueberry jam in the evenings, and she got a nice note back saying it was a very thoughtful offer, but no thanks, because he didn't want to.

It made me feel very grown up to be invited somewhere without Mum and Dad, and I couldn't remember ever having that much money in my pocket before, so after school that Friday I came home, changed out of my uniform, packed a bag and took the Tube to Paddington station for the journey. I was excited at the thought of seeing my brother Jason again and hoped that he wasn't angry with me in the same way he was angry with our parents.

It didn't take long to get to Oxford, about an hour, and I did my best with *Northern Lights* on the way, but the words kept getting mixed up and rearranging themselves before my eyes, and I wished that my brother Jason was there to help me keep them in order. When the train pulled into the station, Aunt Rose was waiting for me at the ticket barrier and she burst into a big smile, screaming so loudly that everyone turned to stare, and I wondered whether I would be better off just turning round and getting the first train home again.

'I knew you'd come,' she said. 'I said to myself, you can always rely on Sam! He won't let you down! It's so good to see you. And you've got so tall since I last saw you! Of course, Aboud was your age when he first came to stay with me – he was only about five foot two when he arrived, but he shot up to nearly six foot before he left. It's your age, I expect.' Aboud was one of the Syrian refugees she'd taken in.

I didn't take much notice of the fact that Aunt Rose's hair was the same colour as Lucozade, because it was a different colour every time I saw her and they were never the normal colours that crayons came in, but strange mixtures of different ones, as if three or four had been melted down in a pot and stirred together afterwards to make something not usually seen in nature. But I was surprised by her outfit, which seemed to have been stitched together from bin bags, hessian cloth and the skin of a dead zebra.

'Do you like it?' she asked, doing a twirl and kicking one foot in the air as if she was a dancer. Her sandal flew off and hit a man on the head, and she had to run over to retrieve it and apologize. 'I made it myself,' she said when she returned to me.

'I thought you might have,' I said.

'Yes, it has that lovely *bespoke* look, doesn't it? The truth is, I missed my calling, Sam. I could have been a fashion designer like that Vivienne Westwood. I designed the costumes once for a production of *A Midsummer Night's Dream* – nothing fancy, just rep – but Albert Finney happened to be in the audience one night at the Durham Playhouse and he came backstage afterwards to say hello to the cast. I was too shy to go over, but I distinctly heard him ask my first husband, your Uncle James, who played Bottom, *Who on earth designed those costumes?* He sounded absolutely astonished by how original they were. It was a very proud moment for me.'

'Who's Albert Finney?' I asked.

'Oh, a tremendous talent. And gorgeous! Before your time, I suppose. Anyway, how was your train journey? Did you talk to anyone nice?'

'Mum and Dad always say that I shouldn't talk to strangers,' I said. 'That they'll only try to put their hands down my trousers.'

'Oh, that's ridiculous,' she said, waving this away. 'Strangers are the most interesting people of all. I met my third husband on a train, you know. Remember Uncle Denzel?'

'Yes,' I said, for he'd been my favourite of Aunt Rose's husbands. He'd taken me to Alton Towers once and bought me as much candyfloss as I wanted. And he knew a lot of rude jokes and loved telling them to me.

'Well, Denzel was a ticket collector on the Cross-Country line, although when I met him he was just a regular passenger like anyone else. We were seated opposite each other and we got talking, and the rest is history. Or it was, for a year or two anyway. Until I threw him out. Oh, come here to me, Sam. Aunt Rose needs a hug!'

'All right,' I said, feeling a little embarrassed as she pulled me tightly into her chest, pressing me so firmly against her enormous breasts that I began to suffocate. I just knew that if this happened anywhere closer to home, my nemesis, David Fugue, would have been walking past and I'd never have heard the end of it.

'Your mum and dad didn't mind you coming?' she asked me as we began to walk towards the car park. She tried to take my hand like I was a little kid, so I shoved it in my pocket.

'I didn't tell them,' I said. 'I just packed a bag, took the Tube to Paddington and caught the train.'

'Oh dear,' she said, stopping for a moment and frowning at me. 'But won't they be worried? Maybe we should phone them when we get home and let them know that you're here. Or we could send a telegram, I suppose. Can you still send telegrams? I don't know if you can. It was all the rage during the war. Not that I was alive during the war, of course. I'm not *that* old. But I've seen the films.'

'It's all right,' I said. 'I left a note on my bed to say where I've gone. If they want me, they know where I am.' I glanced past her, wondering whether my brother Jason had come to the station too and was waiting in the car, but there was no sign of him. Nor could I see Aunt Rose's ancient Morris Minor either but, to my astonishment, there was a horse tied to a fence near the exit. When he saw us coming, he turned his head in our direction and appeared to perform some sort of bow.

'Who on earth would leave a horse here?' I asked, shaking my head in astonishment.

'Oh, that's Bertie Wooster!' said Aunt Rose. 'Didn't I tell you? I sold my car – too expensive to run, and the fumes that go into the atmosphere will kill us all eventually – and bought a horse instead. He doesn't need petrol or diesel and you don't have to tax or insure him.'

I stopped and stared at the horse, then at my aunt and then at the horse again, who was eyeing me suspiciously.

'You rode here on a horse?' I asked in astonishment.

'Yes. What's so strange about that? It's how people always got around in the old days. When Jane Eyre first meets Mr Rochester, he's riding a horse, isn't he? And they're all on them in *Pride and Prejudice*.'

'And you're going to ride him home too?'

'No, I'm going to leave him here to start a family and build a new life all on his own. He'll probably get a job in Marks and Sparks. Of *course* I'm going to ride him home, Sam! And so are you. He's a strong old fellow, aren't you, Bertie Wooster? He can hold both of us.'

I looked at the horse, who sneezed dramatically, and shrugged. Life had become strange enough in recent times; riding a horse back to Aunt Rose's house didn't seem so odd compared to some of the things that had happened at home, so when she picked me up and sort of threw me on to Bertie Wooster's back like I was an old school bag, I did my best to remain calm.

'Well, let's get home, then,' she said as we made our way out on to the road. I felt quite uncomfortable holding on to her waist, but it was either that or fall off, particularly since the cars on the road were beeping at us and Bertie Wooster didn't seem in the least interested in picking up the pace. 'You must be hungry. Boys your age are always hungry, I find.'

'I'm starving,' I agreed.

As Bertie Wooster trotted along, Aunt Rose asked me all the questions grown-ups always ask about school – Did I like it? What was my favourite subject? Who was my best friend? – but when I mentioned Mum and Dad's names, she let out an enormous roar of irritation and it was obvious that she was really annoyed with them both.

'Have they come to their senses yet?' she asked. 'Or are they still behaving like a couple of spoiled children?'

'What do you mean?' I asked.

'Well, they haven't been in touch with their firstborn since Christmas, have they? When they threw the poor child out into the street. What kind of parents would do such a thing?'

'They didn't exactly throw him out,' I said, although I couldn't remember a lot of effort being made on their part to persuade him to stay. 'He chose to leave.'

'Well,' she said, laughing a little, 'it sounds like she didn't have any choice in the matter, having been made to feel miserable every day.'

'Who?' I asked. 'Mum?'

'No, not your mum.'

Bertie Wooster sneezed again and I nearly fell off. 'I thought maybe he'd come to the station with you,' I said.

'Who?'

'My brother Jason.'

'Oh no,' said Aunt Rose. 'I haven't seen Jason since just after New Year's Day.'

'What?' I asked, sitting up so straight that my knees buckled into the horse's side and he pulled up short in protest, turning his head to give me a menacing look. 'You mean he's gone? But where is he? No one's heard from him –'

'Relax, Sam,' she said. 'Everything's fine. You'll be back together shortly, I promise. Look, we're here now.'

Bertie Wooster turned into the driveway of her house and trotted towards a barn that Uncle Bernie had originally built to store his worryingly extensive collection of Nazi war memorabilia. When he stopped, Aunt Rose jumped off before reaching up to help me climb down. I felt completely miserable. If my brother Jason wasn't living with her any more, then what was I even doing there? Were we just going to sit around all night, the two of us, and play Monopoly? And where was he anyway, because he certainly hadn't come home? I pictured him sleeping rough on the streets and the idea frightened me.

'Come on, Sam,' said Aunt Rose as she put the key in her front door. 'Let's go inside.'

Aunt Rose's house was very different from ours. Mum and Dad liked the walls to be snow white and covered with prints of paintings they ordered online from Tate Britain. Also, we had a cleaner who came every Friday morning and knew just how tidy Mum and Dad liked things to be. Compared to that, Aunt Rose's house was a total mess. There were books and newspapers everywhere, half-used scented candles sitting on every table and actual paintings on the wall, although they weren't very good. The only thing I really liked there was her ancient boxer dog, Sandy, who ambled over to say hello and then, recognizing my scent from past visits, did her best to jump up and lick my face, although her tired hips made this difficult.

'You're upstairs in the first room on the right,' said Aunt Rose, 'if you want to put your bag up there.'

I nodded and went upstairs, entering the room that I knew had been Mum's when she was my age. It hadn't changed much since then: the wallpaper looked as if it had been put up back when Henry VIII was king, and the photographs on the wall were of her and Aunt Rose on various holidays with my grandparents. I sat down on the bed and glanced towards the clock. Seven o'clock. I figured that I could pretend to be tired by nine o'clock, go to bed and then get the first train back the next morning. There was no way I was staying for a few days if it was just the two of us. And, anyway, I'd need to tell Mum and Dad that my brother Jason had gone missing and we had to find him. With all her connections, I assumed that Mum would know someone high up in the police force who could help us look for him.

When I came back downstairs again, the kitchen was already filled with the smell of cooking and Sandy was sitting by Aunt Rose's feet, waiting patiently for anything that might fall from the counter.

'I'm making vegetarian spaghetti bolognese,' said Aunt Rose. 'Is that OK?'

'Fine,' I said. 'Could I have meat in mine, though?'

'No. Meat is murder.'

'OK.'

'Jessica should be back soon,' said Aunt Rose. 'She went to the shop to get me some basil.'

I frowned. Jessica? So not only was I going to have to make polite conversation with my aunt all night long, but I was going to have to make it with some random friend of hers too. I felt my heart sink but told myself that I could get through it. This time tomorrow I'd be home again.

'So, Sam,' she said as the vegetables cooked in the pot. They didn't smell great and I wished I'd remembered to bring a Peperami with me. I could have thrown it into my bowl when she wasn't looking. 'I imagine this has been a very difficult few months for you.'

I shrugged. 'It hasn't been easy,' I admitted.

'You've never known anyone who's transgender before, I suppose?'

'No. Have you?'

'Oh, plenty. But back in the day they weren't allowed to be themselves. They had to spend their lives lying to themselves and to the rest of the world. Doesn't sound like much fun, does it?'

I said nothing.

'Have you talked to anyone about it?' she asked eventually.

'Like who?' I asked.

'Well, like your mum and dad, for one. Or for two.'

'No,' I said. 'They don't like to talk about it.'

'Some of your friends maybe?'

I shrugged. 'I don't have many friends, to be honest. And even if I did, I don't think I could. It's not something that's very easy to talk about. How was he anyway? When he was here?'

'He?' she asked, frowning. 'Who is he?'

'My brother Jason.'

'Oh. Well, he was fine when he got here. Upset, of course. Confused. And he needed someone who would just listen and not judge him. I wish that sister of mine could have done that but . . .' She shook her head and looked as if she was trying hard not to say too many negative things in front of me. 'Well, she's your mum,' she said finally. 'I'll bite my tongue. But, still, it's shocking really.'

'He thinks he's a girl,' I said, blurting this out.

'No he doesn't,' replied Aunt Rose.

'He doesn't?' I asked, looking up hopefully. Had he changed his mind? I longed for this to be the case.

'He doesn't *think* he's a girl,' said Aunt Rose. 'She *knows* she's a girl.'

'She's not a she,' I said. 'She's a he.'

'She's not a he because you say she's a he,' said Aunt

Rose. 'If I said you were a plant pot, would that make you a plant pot?'

'It's not the same thing,' I said, shaking my head. 'Not even close.'

'No one wants to be called something they're not, though, do they? What if I said you were a girl? That you were my niece?'

'But I'm not!' I protested. 'I'm a boy. I'm your nephew.'

'I know you are. And you know you are. But Jason felt differently.'

'I don't want to talk about it,' I said. 'I thought he was going to be here. That's the only reason I came.'

'Oh, thanks very much!'

'No, I only meant that –'

'It's all right, Sam. I'm just joking. I get it, you miss him.'

'Of course I do,' I said, feeling tears forming behind my eyes.

'He's been a good brother to you, I can tell.'

'The best,' I said. 'The best ever. And I want him back. I bet you told him that it was all right to be a girl.'

'I didn't tell him anything,' said Aunt Rose, standing up and going over to stir the vegetables and throw some pasta into a pot of boiling water. 'I just let him talk and heard him out, which I have to say I don't think any of you have done. He was in a lot of pain. Couldn't you see that? And he needed someone who was willing to listen.'

'We tried to listen,' I said. 'We all did. It just felt like he'd spent a long time thinking about this himself, and the moment he told us he expected us to understand immediately.'

Aunt Rose sighed and said nothing, but then she seemed to freeze, and when she turned round again she was staring at me with a look of real disappointment on her face.

'Of course,' she said. 'It was you, wasn't it?'

'What was me?' I asked.

'She thought it was your mum or dad who did it, but it was you all the time. She never even suspected you.'

'*What* was me?' I asked again, raising my voice.

'Who cut her ponytail off,' she said. 'You crept in while she was asleep, didn't you? You cut it off and threw it away. Oh, Sam! How could you do such a thing?'

I looked away. I couldn't even be bothered to deny it. 'I was doing him a favour,' I said. 'He looked ridiculous. Everyone was laughing at him.'

'At him or at you, Sam?'

'At *him*,' I insisted.

'But it was her hair. What gave you the right to cut it off?'

'Because he's my brother.'

'No, she's not.'

'He is! And he was trying to look more and more like a girl. So I cut it off because I thought that maybe he would wake up and realize that he looked better with short hair. It's not that big a deal,' I added sulkily.

'Oh, sweetheart,' said Aunt Rose, shaking her head. 'It's a very big deal. It's an *enormous* deal. How can you even think otherwise? The first thing that identified your sister as a girl, something as simple as growing her hair, and you took that away from her. Do you have any idea how much that hurt her? Or how much you stole from her that night?'

'Stop calling him *her*,' I said. 'I hate it.'

'Your feelings matter,' she said. 'I'm not pretending they don't. But they're not the most important thing in this situation. You're upset and you're confused. Of course you are, you're only thirteen. But your sister is going through something much bigger and much more confusing. If you love her, you'll be on her side.'

'I'll always be on my brother Jason's side,' I said, and Aunt Rose said nothing, simply sighed dramatically before turning round and going back to the food.

The phone rang from the hallway and she held her hands in the air, a stirring spoon in each. 'Get that for me, would you, Sam?' she asked. 'And whoever it is, tell them I'll call them back.'

I went out to the hallway, grateful for an escape, and picked up the phone, recognizing my mother's voice immediately.

'Rose? It's Deborah.'

'Hello, Mum,' I said.

'Sam, is that you?' she asked after only a brief pause.

'Yes.'

'Oh, I've lost another son to her, have I?'

'She invited me to stay,' I said.

'Well, she never said anything about it to me,' she replied. 'And neither did you.'

'Yes I did,' I lied. 'I told you the night before last. And you said it was fine for me to go. Also, I left a note on my bed.'

'Did I?' I could tell that she was thinking about it. It was certainly possible that I had told her and, if I had, she probably wouldn't have heard a word anyway. 'Oh yes,' she said. 'That's right, I remember now. Sorry, it must have gone out of my head. There's just so much going on right now.'

'Do you want to talk to Aunt Rose?'

'No, I was calling to see whether she'd heard from you. But now that I know you're safe, I don't need to bother. What's going on there anyway? What are you doing?'

'Nothing much,' I said. 'She's making vegetarian spaghetti bolognese.'

'Oh dear.'

'I know. And she has a friend called Jessica who's coming over later with some basil.'

'Do you want to come home, Sam? Because I can send a car for you if you like. I don't want you to be exposed to anything unsavoury. Bradley's outside and –'

'No, I'm here now,' I said. 'I might as well stay the night.'

'Are you sure?'

'Sandy's here too,' I said. 'And Bertie Wooster.'

'Who?'

'Bertie Wooster. He's a horse.'

'Oh, for pity's sake. And is there . . .' Her voice cracked a little, as if she was trying to fight back tears. 'Is there anyone else there?'

'Jason, you mean?'

'Yes.'

'He's not here at the moment but Aunt Rose says he's still staying. He's probably just out. She says I'll see him later.'

'All right. Well, tell him . . . Tell him . . .'

'Tell him what?' I asked.

'Tell him we miss him.'

'You could come here and tell him yourself if you wanted.'

There was a long pause on the other end of the line as she considered this. 'What time will you be home tomorrow, do you think?' she asked eventually.

'The first train,' I told her. 'The very first train.'

'Fine,' she said. 'Well, see that you are. And don't do this again, Sam, all right? I was worried.'

'Sorry.'

'It's OK. Well, I'll say goodnight, then.'

'Good–' I began, but she'd already put the phone down.

I went back into the kitchen and Aunt Rose turned round. 'Who was that?' she asked.

'Mum,' I said.

'Oh, Lord. I suppose I'm in trouble again?'

'No, I am.'

'Well, better you than me,' she said cheerfully. 'Now, will you lay the table for me please?'

I went over to the drawer and put two place settings down, but Rose turned round and shook her head. 'Three places, Sam,' she said. 'You're forgetting Jessica.'

I went back to the drawer and laid another set out

just as I heard a key in the front door and the sound of someone taking their coat off in the hallway.

'Perfect timing,' said Aunt Rose as she tipped the pasta into a colander and the steam from the water rose into her face.

A moment later the kitchen door opened and a girl a few years older than me walked in. She was wearing blue jeans and a white blouse, and her freshly dyed blonde hair was tied back into a small ponytail. Her face held a light smattering of make-up and her lips wore a pale red gloss. She stopped when she saw me, and I stared at her in astonishment.

'Ah, now this is my fault,' said Aunt Rose, turning round and shrugging her shoulders. 'I thought I would surprise you both. This silliness has gone on for long enough, after all, and it's time to put an end to it.'

'Sam,' said my brother Jason, putting the bag of basil down on the table and looking confused, embarrassed and defiant all at the same time.

'Jason,' I said, uncertain where to look.

'And the first thing that has to stop is this "Jason" nonsense,' said Aunt Rose. 'Jason was left behind in London, all right? This is Jessica. That's the name she wants to be known by. So, when you're under this roof, Sam, please be respectful and call her by that name. Otherwise you and me are going to fall out and you'll be sent outside to sleep in the barn with Bertie Wooster.'

After dinner, my brother Jason asked me whether I wanted to go for a walk with him to catch up. There were lots of fields near Aunt Rose's house, and a river with a bridge over it a few miles away, and we headed in that direction. He went there every day, he told me, because it gave him a good opportunity to think.

'I'm sorry I haven't been in touch more,' he said, and I shrugged my shoulders, pretending that it didn't matter when we both knew that it mattered a great deal. 'I've just been trying to figure everything out, you know.'

'I've been busy too,' I said. 'With school. And homework. I haven't been reading too much, though, since there's no one there to help me.'

He paused and threw me a look, but I didn't acknowledge it. I wanted to hurt him, that was the truth of it.

'Well, I'm sorry about that,' he said. 'Couldn't you ask Mum or Dad, though?'

'They're too busy,' I said. 'Mum's still trying to work her way up the greasy pole. And you know what Dad's like.'

'*Just read what's on the bloody page!*'

I laughed. His impression had been spot-on. 'Yeah,' I said, and then I immediately felt guilty about trying to make *him* feel guilty, so I said, 'I brought *Northern Lights* with me on the train, though. Maybe you could help me with it later?'

'Of course,' he said. 'We can read some when we get home.'

'All right,' I said.

We walked along in silence for a bit, kicking at stones, and once, when we found a discarded, half-pumped football, he kicked it in my direction, a perfect arc over my head, but somehow I jumped perfectly and caught it in my hands, like a real goalkeeper would do.

'Nice!' he said, impressed, and I felt quite proud of myself.

'How long will you be staying here?' I asked as we continued on our way.

'I don't know,' he replied. 'I've just been studying. I'm still sitting my A-levels in June, but it's been easier to study here, with everything that's been going on.'

'And this is still happening?' I asked, looking at his clothes and appearance.

He nodded. 'Yes,' he said. 'Dr Watson has given me lots of books to read on the subject and they've been really helpful. And I go to a support group every Tuesday night.'

'With other boys like you?' I asked.

'Boys who've transitioned to girls. And the other way round. And those who are just thinking about it. I feel very safe there,' he said.

'That's good, I suppose.'

'And I've made some friends.'

'Who all tell you that you're doing the right thing, I suppose.'

'Yes, Sam,' he said calmly. 'That's exactly what they say.'

'And what do you talk about at these meetings?' I asked.

'Whatever we feel like. About how difficult it can be. About unpleasant encounters we might have had. About those small moments of triumph. About the people who accept us exactly as we are, just like Coach O'Brien did. About the people who don't. And about our families, of course.'

I looked at him. 'Have you talked about me?' I asked.

'A little.'

'Did you tell them I'm normal?'

He rolled his eyes. 'I told them that you're not the same as me, if that's what you're worried about. Honestly,

Sam,' he added, his voice rising a little now in irritation, 'there's no need to be quite so nasty.'

'I'm not being nasty!'

'You are. Whether you realize it or not.'

We remained silent for a while then and I could tell that he was annoyed but I didn't think it was my fault. Still, I didn't want to argue so decided I better be the one to talk next.

'Sorry,' I said.

'It's OK.'

'I'm not good with words, you know that.'

'That's only when you're reading, Sam. Don't pretend you don't know how to use them when you're talking. You know exactly what you're saying. Dyslexic people are just as smart as anyone else, they just can't read very well.'

I kicked a few more stones. There wasn't much I could say to that.

'YouTube is good too,' he said eventually.

'What?'

'YouTube. For hearing people tell their stories. Some people aren't good in groups so they record their experiences and put them online. Sometimes, the families of trans people talk too. You should look them up. You might learn something.'

'Parental controls,' I said.

'You haven't figured out how to override them yet?'

'No. Why, did you?'

'Oh yeah. Long ago. I'll show you later. I know all their passwords.'

I laughed. 'Cool,' I said.

'And I suppose the next thing I'll be doing is starting hormone treatment.'

Something inside my stomach twisted a little and I looked at him in concern. 'What does that mean?' I asked. 'Is it like tablets?'

'Tablets, yes. And some shots. It'll be another six months before I'm allowed to do any of that, though. My transition doctor, the one Dr Watson put me in touch with, has to sign off on it when I'm emotionally ready.'

'And what will the tablets do?'

'Things will change for me,' he said. 'Physically, I mean. I'll probably lose some muscle. And I'm told that there'll be a period of mood swings as my body adjusts to the medication. It won't be easy. And then I'll grow . . . you know . . .'

'What?' I asked.

'Oh, come on, Sam,' he said. 'Figure it out.'

'What?' I repeated.

'Breasts,' he said. 'I'll start to grow breasts.'

'Oh,' I said, and I felt a little dizzy, for I couldn't even imagine this. 'Can we sit down for a bit?'

'Of course,' he said, and we sat on the ground and I noticed for the first time that, while my legs had recently started to grow hairs, his were completely smooth. 'I started shaving them,' he said, seeing where I was looking.

'That must feel really weird,' I said.

'It did, at first. Now it feels . . . it feels totally right.'

I looked ahead and could hear the river running somewhere in the distance. There was something else I wanted to ask, but I felt a little embarrassed to put it into words.

'And these tablets . . .' I said. 'Will they make your willy fall off?'

'Oh, for God's sake, Sam,' he said, growing angry now. 'Why is that the only thing you ever think about? Don't you realize that me being the gender I'm supposed to be has absolutely nothing to do with what's going on in my pants? I'm sick of you and your constant willy-talk. You're obsessed.'

'Sorry,' I said, thrown now by how upset he'd grown.

'Are you, though? You're so focused on that, you don't care what's going on in my mind or the rest of my body. Just for once, can you think about something else?'

'All right,' I said, holding my hands up defensively. 'I said I'm sorry.'

'Yeah, well,' he muttered, and we continued walking for a while without saying another word.

'I suppose what I'm most worried about,' he said finally, his tone calm again, 'is how it will feel to live as a woman every day. My face is quite masculine so I think people will always be looking at me on the streets and there'll always be people calling me names. For the rest of my life.'

I felt a burst of anger inside me. A bunch of strangers making fun of him when they didn't know how brilliant and kind he was. It made me want to be by his side forever, as if I was the older brother and not him. 'How will you cope with that?' I asked.

'I don't know,' he admitted. 'I guess I have to hope that attitudes change. That the world is more kind than cruel. Also, well, I don't know if anyone will ever fall in love with me.'

'Of course they will,' I said. 'You're amazing. You've always been amazing. What kind of idiot wouldn't be able to see that?'

'She'll have to be very understanding. It's going to be very, very difficult, I know that for sure.'

'And yet you still want to go through with it?' I asked.

'I don't have a choice,' he said. 'Otherwise, my entire life will be a lie. And I can't live like that. No matter what happens, I have to be myself.'

'And this . . . Jessica business?' I asked, for Aunt Rose had spent the entire evening addressing him by this name. 'Is that forever too?'

'Yes,' he said. 'You can start calling me it if you like.'

I thought about it but shook my head. 'I can't just yet,' I said. 'I'm sorry, I'm getting there. I'm really trying. But you're my brother Jason and I just can't think of you in any other way. You'll always be my brother Jason.'

He sighed and looked away, shaking his head. 'But I'm not,' he said. 'Do you still not get it, Sam? I'm not. Not any more.'

8

The Betrayal

I finally understood why Mum and Dad had been working so hard when the Prime Minister resigned and, before he even got to the end of his statement, the news crews arrived outside our house, waiting for Mum to make hers. She left them standing in the cold for an hour before stepping outside with Dad, having made it very clear to me that I wasn't to follow them or watch through a window. And so I turned on the television and watched her there instead, which felt a little strange, considering all I had to do was lean back in the armchair and I could see both of them standing on the top step while the photographers took their pictures and the journalists roared their questions.

'This is a very sad day for our country,' said Mum,

looking sombre but determined, and her voice came from both the television and from behind me in stereo sound. 'My dear friend the Prime Minister has given extraordinary service to this country for more than seven years now, and it is with a heavy heart that I see him decide that the time has come to depart for new challenges. I want to wish him and his family well in the adventures that lie before them once he has left office. Over the past few hours, I have been overwhelmed by calls and messages from parliamentary colleagues and friends asking me to consider putting myself forward for the leadership and, while it has never been a position that I have sought or wanted, it seems clear that we are at a crucial juncture in the story of our island nation and that the best way I can serve my country is to allow this to happen. I shall leave it to others to decide whether or not they can support me.'

The journalists all started shouting together, but she simply smiled and stepped back into the hallway, though not before offering them one more opportunity to take photographs of her and Dad waving outside our own number ten. Once inside again, and with the door closed firmly behind her, she looked at the dozen or so party colleagues who had gathered in the hallway for reassurance, and each one declared that she had been outstanding, absolutely outstanding.

'Do you think anyone else will put themselves forward?' she asked, looking from one face to the other anxiously. 'While I'm not opposed to the idea of a coronation, a victory would be better, don't you think? I'd prefer the mandate that would confer.'

'There's only Joe,' said Dad. 'And we'll know his intentions within the hour, I expect. If he declines, then it's you. But even if he goes for it, I think you'll win anyway. You have the numbers.'

'Yes, I think so too,' said Mum. 'But, still, it might not be such a bad thing for him to run. If he was to lose graciously, then that could serve us both well. Should we get that message to him, do you think? Let him know there'd be a good job in it for him?'

'Let's just wait and see,' said Dad. 'Sam, don't touch that remote. No one changes the channel until we find out what happens next. Half of London's media are on their way to Joe's front door right now. He's got to say something soon.'

It had been a couple of weeks since I'd left Aunt Rose's house and I talked to my brother Jason on the phone every few days and always asked him to come home, but he always said that he couldn't, not yet. Talking to him felt like old times and I started asking him questions about how he was feeling and began to understand that, while things on the outside might be changing for him, the person on the inside was still the same.

But something else had changed in my life during that time, something that I had told absolutely no one about: I had a girlfriend. Sort of. It had happened by chance – I definitely hadn't been looking for one – but nevertheless I was very happy about it, especially as I'd just turned fourteen and found that, suddenly, I couldn't stop thinking about girls all day long, from the moment I woke up until the moment I went to sleep. There were quite a few girls I liked, but each one for different reasons.

TEN GIRLS I LIKED AND THE REASONS I LIKED THEM

1. Penny Wilson, who used to go out with my brother Jason, because I could never seem to forget the day I'd discovered them lying on his bed together and the pink bra she wore underneath her white blouse.
2. Dominique Fugue, the older sister of my nemesis, David Fugue, who had lovely skin the colour of

caramel. I thought about her a lot and tried not to hold her brother against her.

3. Kate Middleton. I didn't know why, I'd just always liked looking at pictures of her.

4. Sandra, a girl who worked on the tills in my local WHSmith. I didn't know her surname because it didn't say it on her name badge, but she had nice eyes and was always reading behind the counter.

5. Cheryl Tweedy. Obviously.

6. Miss Whiteside, my maths teacher, who was from South Africa. I'd liked her for ages, especially the way she talked, and sometimes she leaned over me while I was doing sums, and then I could smell her perfume and I'd nearly pass out.

7. Jivika Ghosh, who was in the same year as my brother Jason and was friends with him too. She was just incredibly hot, and whenever she saw me she'd say, 'Hi, Sam!' and I'd blush like crazy, but I loved that she knew my name.

8. Saoirse Ronan, whose name I can pronounce (it's *Seer-sha*).

9. The girl on page 126 of the June 2017 issue of *Vogue*, which was my favourite issue of all time and always seemed to be at the top of my special

box with the lock and key at the back of my
wardrobe.

10. My new girlfriend.

It had all started the day after I'd returned to London
from Aunt Rose's. I'd walked down to my local park
and was sitting by the lake, trying to read some more of
Northern Lights, putting my fingers beneath the words
and sounding them out when necessary, when I heard a
voice call out my name.

'Sam,' she said. 'It is Sam, isn't it?'

I turned round and felt my stomach do somersaults.

'Laura,' I said, my voice rising about eighteen octaves,
so I coughed and said her name again, this time really
deep, as if I was Morgan Freeman. I hadn't seen her
since Christmas Day, but I'd been thinking about her a
lot since then.

'You remembered my name!'

'Of course I did,' I said. 'You remembered mine too.'

'True,' she said, laughing. 'What are you doing?'

I shrugged and nodded in the direction of the lake.
'Not much,' I said, closing my book. 'Trying to work
out why the ducks over there seem happier than me.'

She smiled and sat down beside me. She was sitting so
close that our knees were almost touching. 'I came to

look at the gardens,' she said. 'Have you seen them recently?'

'I've walked through them,' I said, scrunching up my face. 'I probably haven't really *looked*, though. Not the way you'd look anyway.'

'This time of year is magical,' she said, her face lighting up now. 'When all the new buds appear.'

'Have you always been into flowers?' I asked.

'Yes, for as long as I can remember,' she said. 'But not just flowers. Plants too. And trees. My dad owns a book called *Meetings with Remarkable Trees* and it's just pictures of all these great trees from around the world and I look at them all the time. One day I want to visit them all.'

I glanced around. There were trees everywhere, but I had to admit I'd never really taken much notice of any of them before. Still, they looked as if they'd been there for centuries and I wondered how often they'd seen other boys – boys my age, I mean – sitting around feeling really sorry for themselves just like I was doing.

'That was awful, wasn't it?' Laura said, after I hadn't spoken for a while. 'Christmas Day, I mean. All that politics. And my dad kissing up to your mum so she'll give him a good job when she becomes PM.'

'You don't think that's going to happen, do you?' I asked. 'I've been praying that it won't.'

'Really? I would have thought you'd want it.'

'I barely see her as it is,' I said. 'If she becomes prime minister, then that's it. The next time we meet, it'll probably be on my wedding day.'

'Oh yes?' said Laura, giggling. 'Got your eye on someone, have you?'

I laughed and blushed a little. 'Figure of speech,' I said.

'Well, I hate to tell you this,' she said, 'but it seems like a foregone conclusion. Unless something comes along to ruin her plans. Still, it might be sort of interesting living in Ten Downing Street.'

'I'm perfectly happy with ten Rutherford Road,' I said.

We sat in silence for a few minutes, looking at the water, and then an old lady walked past, fishing in her bag for some slices of bread to feed to the ducks. They swam towards her eagerly, their heads dipping into the water in search of every crumb, and a few even stepped out, standing by her feet, waiting for something to fall on dry land.

'How's your brother doing?' Laura asked.

'My brother?'

'Yes, I didn't get to meet him, remember? He was

helping out in that homeless shelter on Christmas Day. Or so your mother claimed, but I didn't believe her.'

'Oh yes,' I said, and, without meaning to, I started to laugh.

'What's so funny?' she asked.

'Nothing,' I said.

'Come on, there must be something.'

I turned to look at her and our eyes met. I felt I could talk to her. I felt I could trust her.

'You were right,' I said. 'He wasn't volunteering at all. Mum just made that up.'

'So where was he?' she asked.

I leaned forward and placed my head in my hands. I wasn't crying – I wasn't even close to crying – I just needed to block myself off from the world for a few moments. She didn't say anything to interrupt the silence, though, and I was glad of that. When I sat back up again, I started to speak, although I didn't look directly at her, staring at the water instead.

'Last summer,' I said, 'he told us that he didn't want to be a boy any more. Or rather that he didn't think he was a boy any more. Or that he'd ever been one. He thought he was a girl. I know that sounds ridiculous but –'

'It doesn't sound ridiculous at all,' said Laura quietly, reaching out and taking my hand, and it felt great when she did that. Her skin was really soft, and I liked her fingers being wrapped around my own.

'Mum and Dad don't want him to be a girl, so they sent him to a psychologist who looks like the singer out of Coldplay and they told him that he had to stop saying it, but he wouldn't, and so he left home just before Christmas and he hasn't come back since. He's been staying with my Aunt Rose, who has a horse called Bertie Wooster, and she calls him Jessica because that's how he wants to be known now, and he dresses like a girl and wears perfume and has a new ponytail even though I cut the old ponytail off, and now everyone at home pretends that he doesn't exist and they haven't spoken about him in ages.'

And then I did start crying, but not very much, just a few tears, and I made sure to use the hand that Laura wasn't holding to wipe them away. We said nothing for a very long time, and eventually she broke the silence.

'Did you ever think that something was a really big deal,' she asked, 'but then later, when it was all over, you wondered why you ever thought it was such a big deal in the first place?'

I turned to her and frowned. 'Sort of,' I said. 'Not really. I don't know. Huh?'

'About eight years ago,' she said, 'when I was only

six, my dad left my mum for a bit. He was seeing someone else and they even had a baby together, my half-brother Damian. I was just a kid back then and it was really upsetting, because my family was falling apart. It was in all the papers at the time, since Dad had just been promoted to the Shadow Cabinet and it was a real scandal. Anyway, I thought it was the worst thing that had ever happened in the history of the world, but eventually it all calmed down and my parents even got back together in the end, and I see my little brother all the time and he's great. I can't even imagine life without him. He's my favourite person *ever*. But at the time it seemed like such a massive drama, and eventually it just . . .' She thought about it for a moment. 'I don't know,' she said. 'It just passed.'

'I didn't know any of that,' I said.

'Well, there's no reason why you would. It was all so long ago anyway. But my point is that, even if something seems like a big deal one day, it usually passes and you end up looking back, wondering what all the drama was for. Maybe that's how it will be with your brother. Obviously, it's a huge strain right now, and really upsetting. For you, for your parents and particularly for him. But imagine if it all worked out fine and everyone accepted what he's said and he found happiness and it was five years from now and everybody was happy again. Wouldn't you look back to today and ask yourself, what was all the fuss about?'

I shrugged. 'Maybe,' I said. 'But I'm not sure it will all work out that easy.'

'Why not?'

'I just don't think so,' I said.

'But why not?' she insisted. 'What's wrong with people just working things out and deciding to be happy?'

'You make it sound easy,' I said. 'But everything is falling apart. My whole family. I don't even know where *I'm* going to be living in a few months' time, let alone where *he's* going to be living.'

'Sam,' she said, and her voice was much quieter now. She sounded very serious. 'I have something very important to tell you.'

'All right,' I said.

'No, turn this way. You have to be looking right at me when I tell you this because it's something you're going to remember for the rest of your life.'

I did as Laura asked, turning and staring directly at her. Our faces weren't very far apart and I felt a bit dizzy as I looked at her. At that moment, the rest of the world didn't even exist. 'So?' I asked. 'What did you want to tell me?'

'This,' she said, leaning forward and kissing me. Her lips touched mine, and even though I was completely astonished, I found that I knew exactly what to do. I let my body and my face relax and I kissed her back. And then, almost as soon as the kiss had started, it came to an end. 'When I said your brother was cute on Christmas Day,' she said, 'I also said that you looked like him, remember? But he's, like, really old. What I was trying to say was that *you* were cute.'

'Oh,' I said, sitting back and feeling completely amazed. I couldn't help it, I had a stiffy and I was worried that she'd look down and think I was a total sicko. 'Thank you.'

'You don't need to thank me,' she said, smiling.

'OK.'

'Was that your first kiss?'

'Of course not,' I said, trying to laugh with as much confidence as I could possibly muster. 'I've kissed loads of girls. Hundreds of them. Thousands, probably.'

'Really?'

'No. Just you.'

'OK.'

'What about you?' I asked.

'I've kissed one other boy. But he wasn't very nice to me afterwards so I don't want to talk about him.'

'All right,' I said, taking her hand again and squeezing

it tight, and then we said nothing for a long time, just sat and watched the ducks, and after a while I realized that she had laid her head on my shoulder and, even though I desperately wanted to kiss her again, I also didn't want her to move from where she was, so I said nothing and she said nothing, and all in all it was a perfect afternoon.

'You won't tell anyone, will you?' I asked her when we parted a couple of hours later at the Tube station, after a lot more kissing and a plan to meet again at the weekend and go to see a film together. 'About my brother, I mean. You won't say a word?'

'Of course not,' she said, making that zip sign across her mouth. 'My lips are sealed.'

My mum's political future was back on the agenda at home as more and more people arrived at the house – people from the party, people from the constituency – and almost everyone seemed to have a phone pressed to their ear or was holding an iPad in their hand. I was standing by Mum when an official came over and took her by the arm.

'I've just heard,' he said. 'From Joe's people. He's not going to stand.'

Mum took a step back and put a hand to her mouth. 'So it's over?' she asked. 'It's just me? I'm unopposed?'

'It looks that way,' he said. 'Joe is about to make his statement and then, if it's as I'm hearing, the party is ready to fall in line behind you. There's no question. Of course, he'll want a big job –'

'Of course,' said Mum, looking away, and I could see that she was lost in thought about the future. 'And that's only fair. But not too big, I think. Nothing where he could cause me any trouble in the long run. So not one of the big four. Health, perhaps. Or defence.'

'Yes, or –'

A cry went up from the living room and I could hear one of the party workers calling us all over. We dashed in and stared at the television set, no one saying a word for a few moments.

'I don't get it,' said Mum eventually, frowning a little as she looked at the screen. 'That's not Joe's house.'

'It must be,' said one of the party workers. 'Why else would the news crews be there?'

'No, I've been to Joe's house,' insisted Mum. 'It looks nothing like that.'

'Then whose house is it?' asked Dad.

'I'm not sure. I vaguely recognize it but –'

And then the room fell silent as Joe stepped outside alone and stood before the cameras. He held some pages in his hand and repeated, practically word for word, everything Mum had said earlier about the country being in the Prime Minister's debt. But then he diverted a little.

'And now the moment comes for the party, and the country, to find a new leader,' he said. 'As you all know, I have served in many different departments over my years in government and have been honoured to do so, and, perhaps, if I was ten years younger, I would feel that I was willing to take on the ultimate challenge of putting my name forward for prime minister. But I am not ten years younger and I must be honest with you and say that I feel my time has passed.'

Mum looked at Dad and he put his arm around her and pulled her close as everyone cheered, and only when Joe started speaking again did the room fall into a hush.

'It's at moments like this, of course,' he continued, 'when we are potentially looking at the next ten years' governance of our country, that we must ask ourselves, who is the best man for the job? Which is the right face for our country? Do we want to continue in our great traditions or open ourselves up to a modernism that, for some, is both worrying and objectionable?'

'What on earth is he babbling about?' asked Dad, but Mum said nothing, and I could see her calculating forward a few steps. A slight smile crossed her lips when she saw what happened on the screen next and, while everyone else in the room gasped, she closed her eyes for a moment, an expression on her face that said, *Of course!*

For, from the doorway behind Joe, three people emerged. Bobby and Stephanie Brewster, our Christmas Day guests, and Laura, their daughter, my girlfriend, looking more pale and beautiful than ever but trembling, I noticed, and close to tears. Her whole body was shaking.

'And that is why,' continued Joe, 'despite the extraordinary talents of Deborah Waver, who has so much to contribute to our public life over the years to come, it seems to me that Bobby Brewster is the man to lead our government and our country. Now, you all know Bobby, a dedicated public servant, a man of the people, a family man whose family, if I may be forgiven for employing such a politically incorrect term, is a *normal* family.'

'Now, now,' said Bobby, laughing a little and shaking his head.

'No, I don't mean anything by that, of course,' said Joe. 'And let me be clear when I say that Deborah Waver's family problems, particularly the psychiatric issues of her elder son – who *is* her son, no matter what he might think – play no part in my decision to support

Bobby. I just think that it's important that we hold on to some of our standards. And so, ladies and gentlemen, I give you the next Prime Minister of Great Britain and Northern Ireland, Bobby Brewster.'

Bobby stepped forward to the sound of camera shutters and, although he spoke for almost five minutes, I heard almost nothing he said. The room was in silence and I could see both Mum and Dad trembling slightly in fury and disbelief.

'Well, that's it,' said Mum, when he had finished speaking and the family had gone back indoors. She turned to look around the room. 'It's over.'

And not a single person contradicted her.

I went out into the hallway, intending to go to my room, which was about the only part of the house unoccupied by party workers, and as I did so the telephone rang. I stared at it, not wanting to answer it, certain that it would be a journalist looking for a comment. But it continued for so long that the sound was becoming awful, so I lifted it to my ear.

'Hello?' I said.

'Sam,' said a panicked voice at the other end. 'It's me, Laura. Sam, I'm so sorry. I didn't mean to tell anyone, and I never would have if I thought any of this would happen. I just mentioned it to Mum because I wanted to know what she thought, and she seemed to understand because she said –'

I didn't hear any more of what she said. I'd already hung up and was walking slowly up to the stairs to my room, where I locked the door behind me and swore that I would never trust anyone again, not for as long as I lived.

9

A Pretend Boy

1. That I was thirteen (*Sun*). No, I was fourteen by then.

2. That Mum and Dad had met at a party meeting and Mum had asked Dad out first (*Mirror*). No, they met in the foyer of a theatre and Dad asked Mum out.

3. That we'd gone through eleven au pairs in six years and 'every one of those poor girls left after outrageous demands had been made of her' (*The Times*). Close, but not entirely accurate. One of those poor girls, after all, was a poor boy.

4. That Dad was a big Boyzone fan (*Irish Times*). No, he's a big Westlife fan. And there's a difference.

5. That Mum had been plotting against the Prime Minister since the start of her parliamentary career (*Guardian*). No, I overheard her saying to Dad that she only started plotting when she got into the Cabinet.

6. That Aunt Rose had affairs with both Mick Jagger and Mick Jagger's son. That she tried to kill a man in a pub for talking about the benefits of wind turbines. That she's pen pals with nine different men on Death Row in America (*Daily Mail*). I actually don't know if any of that's true, but I suppose it might be.

7. That I was a member of the mountaineering club at school (*Telegraph*). No, and I have literally no idea where they got that one from. We don't even have a mountaineering club at school. That I know of, anyway.

8. That my brother Jason was suffering from a psychological disorder and Mum and Dad had consulted professionals about having him sectioned in a home for mad people (*Daily Express*). No, they'd never have done that.

9. That Mum and Dad had bought 10 Rutherford Road, waiting for the day when they could get their photos taken outside it before moving into 10 Downing Street (*Observer*). No, the house belonged to my dad's parents and he inherited it from them.

10. That neither Mum nor Dad had spoken to Jason in over two months (*Sun, Mirror, The Times, The Irish Times, Guardian, Daily Mail, Telegraph, Financial Times, Observer*).

OK, it's really nine things that the newspapers said about my family that weren't true.

There's something very strange about being in a classroom where everyone knows that your brother believes he's a girl, your mother is running for prime minister and the papers are writing stories about your family every day. No one knows quite how to talk to you, but at the same time they're desperate to hear exactly what's going on at home. They think you're a freak, but even so they're envious of the excitement going on in your life when their own life is pretty boring. I found myself wishing that they'd all just leave me alone. I had enough people staring at me when I walked in and out of our house every day without it taking place at school too. Invisibility was always the best option.

Laura phoned me several times in the two weeks leading up to the party vote, but I wouldn't take her calls. Our cleaner moved into the guest room to help out with breakfasts, lunches and dinners as my parents were so busy, and she took control of the phone, eventually telling my now ex-girlfriend that if she didn't stop calling the police would be informed. I felt bad when I overheard that particular conversation because I missed Laura, and I *really* missed kissing her, but I just couldn't find it within myself to forgive her for what she'd done.

Although I didn't want Mum to become prime minister, I knew that it had been her ambition for a long time, so I began to hope that she'd succeed. After all, she was very good at her job and wanted to make the country a better place in which to live. It was obvious, really, considering how hard she worked, and how late she stayed up every night reading her documents. The one sentence I'd heard her say so many times when discussing policies with her advisers was, *But will it make people's lives better?*

During those two weeks, my job was to help as much as possible, to take all the empty bottles and food containers out to the rubbish bins twice a day, to not make a nuisance of myself and – on pain of death – to say nothing, *absolutely nothing*, to the journalists standing outside.

Under other circumstances, I would have started cycling to school again now, because the weather was so much better, but as we were receiving so much attention Bradley picked me up every morning at eight o'clock, and he took no prisoners as he strode up the drive, pushing past reporters left and right and practically lifting me from the doorway before tossing me into the back seat of the car.

'Don't you ever want to tell them to take a hike?' he asked me, four days into this interminable drama. 'If they were in my drive, I'd turn the hose on them. I would!'

I laughed. I quite liked that idea. 'Mum would kill me if I did that,' I said.

'She would get over it,' said Bradley.

'There's only a few days to go now anyway,' I told him. 'Then she'll either have won or she'll have lost. And after that I suppose they'll go away.'

'Not if she wins,' he said. 'You'll be stuck with them forever if that happens.'

I said nothing.

The newspapers were starting to write more and more

stories about my brother Jason and they did everything they could to make him sound like a total freak. *Waver's son's a trannie!* said one. *Waver's boy's a girl! Waver kid wavering on gender!* It went on and on. And, although every reporter was trying to track him down, there was still no sight or sound of him, and Aunt Rose said that he had gone to stay with a friend of hers until the fuss died away. Actually, there were one or two papers who took his side and published articles about young people who'd made the same decision about their own life, and when I read them it seemed like things had worked out fine for them in the long run.

'Should we ask the police to look for him?' said Mum on one of those rare occasions when she, Dad and I were alone, late at night, and all the advisers had gone home and the journalists had packed up for the night.

'I'm not sure there's any point,' said Dad. 'It's not as if he's been kidnapped or anything. We knew he'd gone to Rose's and now we know that Rose has sent him somewhere else. She says he's perfectly safe but she won't tell us unless Jason says it's OK. I'm sure he's not in any danger and that he'll get in touch when he's ready.'

'But I'm worried about him,' said Mum, a slight catch in her throat now.

'So am I,' said Dad, looking down at the floor, and

the silence that existed between the three of us began to feel embarrassing.

'If you were all that worried about him,' I said finally, 'then you wouldn't have thrown him out.'

'But we didn't –' began Dad, but Mum put a hand gently on his arm to silence him.

'We may not have thrown him out as such,' she said quietly, 'but we made it impossible for him to stay here. It's our fault that he left and, if anything happens to him, then that will be our fault too.'

And then she did something that always upset me. She put her head in her hands and started to cry. I stared at her in shock, not quite knowing what to do, but after a moment Dad put his arms around her and, to my horror, he started crying too, and all I wanted to do was run screaming from the room.

'Stop crying,' I said, but they ignored me. 'Stop crying!' I repeated, raising my voice now and standing up. 'It won't do any good.'

'He's right,' said Dad, drying his eyes. 'We need to be more proactive.'

'We should have listened to him more,' said Mum. 'We should have tried to understand. What will all this be for –' and here she picked up a newspaper with her photograph next to Bobby Brewster's on the front page – 'if Jason isn't here to share it too? We drove him away, that's the truth of it. How the hell can I say that I would take care of sixty million people if I can't even take care of one?'

Dad started to cry again, at which point she took his hand in hers and held it tight. They were speaking to each other as if I wasn't even in the room.

'Do you remember when we first met?' she asked.

'Of course I do. In that theatre on Shaftesbury Avenue.'

'And when we started dating, all the things we talked about? All the plans we had for the future and how we were going to change the country for the better? Even if I win, which is virtually impossible now anyway, it won't make Jason come home. It might only drive him further away. Oh, God, Alan, what have we done to him? How could we have been so careless with our own son?'

And then they didn't say anything else, just started to cry again, and I went to my room, but not before opening the door to my brother Jason's room and looking around at his posters, his books and the bed that hadn't been slept in for ages.

'Where are you?' I asked out loud.

She was waiting for me when I left school, halfway between my house and the park. I think I noticed her even before she saw me and, while there was a part of me that wanted to turn round and find another way home, I knew I couldn't do it because I missed her so much. She was my girlfriend, after all. Or she had been for a couple of weeks. The first girl I'd ever kissed. And it wasn't just that I wanted to kiss her again – although I did, a lot – it was also that I liked her.

'Sam,' she said as I came close, and I stopped on the pavement, holding my head low for a few moments before deciding to walk over to her.

'We probably shouldn't be meeting,' I said. 'If any journalists see us together –'

'I'm sick of journalists,' she said. 'Aren't you?'

'Of course I am,' I replied, for I dreaded running the gauntlet of them every time I tried to go in or out of the house. 'It's got to the point where I know most of their names.'

'Me too,' she said. 'They show up at six o'clock every morning and just start screaming at us whenever one of us opens the front door.'

I smiled and felt an urge to shout at her, walk away from her, hug her and kiss her all at once. In the end, I just asked her whether she wanted to go for a walk in the park and, to my relief, she agreed.

'You've been ignoring all my calls,' she said as we

walked around the flower beds, and she didn't even seem to be paying attention to them, despite the fact that the spring plants were coming into bloom. She was just looking at me. 'I've stopped ringing. There's only so much humiliation a girl can take, you know.'

'What I told you . . .' I began. 'I told you that in secret. It was private. I confided in you, Laura.'

'I know,' she said. 'And I honestly didn't mean to betray you. I wanted to help you, that's the truth, but knew that I couldn't if I didn't really understand it. So I went to the library to read about it, but I couldn't find anything. And when I went on the internet, all the sites were blocked.'

'Everyone knows how to get around them!'

'Do you?'

'Yes, my brother Jason showed me.'

'Well, I don't *have* a brother Jason, Sam.'

'It's not porn anyway,' I said. 'So it shouldn't be blocked. It's people's lives.'

'I know, but that's the internet for you. Anyway, that's when I told Mum. I wanted her to tell me what she knew about it. I thought it was just between us, but then she told Dad. And I suppose he decided that it was something he could use to win the leadership for himself. I never even knew he was interested in it.

He always said that he was planning on supporting your mum.'

'That's what she thought too.'

'I think he just saw a chance and took it.'

'Great.'

'If it's any consolation, Sam,' she said, 'I'm furious with him.'

'It's not much,' I said. 'But thank you for saying it, I suppose.'

We said nothing for a while then, just walked along, and I desperately wanted to take her hand, but I couldn't bring myself to do it. I was still angry with her, and with myself for confiding in her, and I wanted her to understand that.

'How is he anyway?' she asked eventually, breaking the silence.

'Who?'

'Your brother Jason.'

'I don't know,' I said, shrugging my shoulders.

'You haven't seen him?'

'No.'

'Or heard from him?'

'We've talked on the phone, but not in more than a week. Not since the newspapers got the story.'

'So he's not still at your aunt's, then?'

I shook my head and told her everything we knew. That Aunt Rose had sent him off to one of her hippy friends but that he'd be back soon. The only thing we knew for sure was that, when he went, he was dressed as Jessica and not Jason. And that's what worried me the most. I knew that there were people out there who wouldn't think twice about beating someone like him up if they saw him late at night on the streets. I'd read about it in the newspapers. And if his own brother would cut his ponytail off, then what would a complete stranger do to him?

'He can't have just vanished into thin air,' said Laura, shaking her head.

'Of course he hasn't,' I said, raising my voice now in frustration. 'He's safe, we know that, but he won't talk to us. Because his own family treated him like he was a freak. He must have read about Mum in the papers and thought he should stay away or he'd cost her votes in the party election. I might never see him again, and he was ... he was the best big brother ...' I sat down on a bench and felt my hands curl into fists. I wanted to punch something. Or have someone come over and punch me. Anything to take away this terrible pain that I felt.

'I'm sure he'll come back,' said Laura.

'How can you be sure of that?' I asked, shouting at her now. 'How can anyone be? You've never even met him. You don't know him at all. You don't know what's going through his mind. I should have been there for him and I wasn't. He was my brother Jason,' I said. 'And what did it matter if he wanted to have a ponytail or wear a dress or put on make-up or call himself Jessica? It didn't matter at all. I let him down, that's what happened. This is all my fault.'

'No, it's mine,' she said, sitting down next to me and taking me in her arms, and I let her and, despite all the pain I was feeling and the regret that was going through my mind, once she put her arms around me I got another stiffy. I hated myself for it but there was nothing I could do. Those stiffies had minds of their own.

'Just leave me alone,' I said, pushing her away. 'If you hadn't spoken to your mum –'

'I've told you how sorry I am,' she said.

'I don't care, Laura,' I said, standing up and drying my eyes. I could feel the next sentence forming in my mind and I didn't want to say it, but it came out anyway. 'I don't want to see you again. Ever.'

'If I could go back and change things –'

'But you can't.'

'I didn't mean it.'

'And yet you did it.'

She stared at me for a long time and then nodded. 'All right,' she said, standing up. 'But for what it's worth, Sam, I'm really sorry. I really am.'

'I just want him back,' I said, succumbing to her kindness now and feeling such pain in my stomach that I was practically doubled over. I opened my mouth, expecting a great cry of pain to emerge, but there was nothing there. Just silence. Just loneliness.

When I got back to the house that evening, there seemed to be even more journalists gathered outside than usual. The party vote was only two days away and the newspapers were pretty unanimous in their opinions: Bobby Brewster was going to win and become the next prime minister. And Mum would most likely be returned to the back benches. It seemed that there wasn't a single television news programme or radio show that didn't have an opinion on the subject of transgenderism and, although my brother Jason had two parents, almost every reporter blamed Mum for what they described as his 'eccentricity'. Even those newspapers who were supportive of my brother Jason still found small ways to blame Mum, as if her being ambitious and having a career somehow meant that she should be held responsible.

The strange thing was that it didn't matter who wrote the column – a man or a woman – the line was always the same. That Mum was at fault and Dad was a weakling because he was Mum's private secretary. That if she'd simply stayed at home all these years and made a few shepherd's pies, then everything would have turned out differently. Mum told me not to read the articles, they were all rubbish, but I couldn't help it. I needed to know what they were writing about her. About us.

In the kitchen, I found Mum and Dad seated next to each other at the table, surrounded by party workers, reading a three-page document and making notes on it.

'Best go to your room, Sam,' said one of the younger workers, and I turned to him, feeling furious about being barred from my own kitchen.

Before I could say a word, Mum shouted at the top of her voice, 'No!'

The entire room fell silent and everyone turned to look at her.

'That's my son,' she said. 'And I'm not going to make the same mistake twice. Would you step aside, please, and let him through!'

The crowd parted and I walked between her and

Dad, looking from one to the other and lowering my voice so that I could keep our conversation private. 'What's going on?' I asked.

'It's over,' she said. 'I'm conceding.'

'But why?' I asked. 'The vote is only two days away and –'

'And I can't win. So it's better to bow out gracefully now and let Bobby take over.'

I nodded. 'Will he give you a good job at least?'

She shook her head and laughed. 'I don't think so,' she said. 'Anyway, I'm not so sure I want one any more.'

I felt a great weight of sadness building inside me. Everything had gone wrong. My brother Jason hadn't been seen in ages, Mum was about to step away from the only job she'd ever really wanted, Dad would probably be out of work, and what would happen to us all then?

'So, here's what I'm going to do, Sam,' she continued. 'I'm going to go outside and address the media and tell them my decision. It's going to be a circus for another couple of days, I'm afraid. Until Bobby's in Number Ten and has announced his cabinet. But I'm pretty sure everything will calm down after that. I'm sorry about all this disruption, I really am.'

'That's OK,' I said. 'But are you sure? You might never get a chance to be prime minister again.'

'I haven't seen my firstborn in almost three months,' she said, swallowing quickly, and I could see how close to tears she was. 'And I've only now realized how much damage I've caused to this family. So, quite honestly, Sam, the answer is yes. I don't think I've ever been as sure of anything in my life.'

As she and Dad stood up, I nodded and was going to go upstairs to my room but then decided against it. 'Can I come out with you?' I asked.

'I don't think so, Sam,' said Dad. 'They're going to be screaming questions at your mum and it'll be very unpleasant.'

'That's why I want to be there,' I said, looking up at Mum. 'I want to be standing next to you when they say all their mean things. Can't we ask everyone else to stay inside?'

'Everyone else?' she asked.

'All these people,' I said, looking around the room at the crowd of party workers, almost none of whom I recognized and absolutely none of whom had ever bothered to show any interest in me.

Mum looked at Dad and shrugged her shoulders. 'What the hell,' she said. 'All right, everyone, it will just be me, my husband and Sam facing the media.'

A ripple of disappointed conversation filled the room;

they knew that whoever was standing closest to Mum would show up on every news report for the next twenty-four hours.

'Secretary of State,' said one young man in a dark blue suit who I'd overheard being rude to our cleaner a few times. 'Perhaps if I was to join you for moral –'

'You three go out,' said a voice as someone stepped in from the hallway, 'and I'll shut the door behind you. The rest of you, stay exactly where you are or there'll be trouble.'

I looked across and there was Bradley, our driver, glaring around with an expression on his face that said, if anyone tried to cross him, they would probably live to regret it.

'Thank you, Bradley,' said Mum as we made our way out into the corridor. She turned to Dad on her left-hand side and then to me on her right and smiled. 'Are we ready?' she asked.

'We still have a full life ahead of us, Deborah,' said Dad, leaning into Mum's ear. 'We'll get past this, I promise we will. And once we have, then our first priority will be –'

'Bringing our child home,' said Mum.

'Exactly.'

She smiled and kissed his cheek, then took each of

us by a hand and we made our way towards the front door.

Once we were outside, I found it almost impossible to keep my eyes open, the cameras were flashing so quickly. At least eight television cameras were pointed in Mum's direction and perhaps a dozen radio microphones. They jostled with each other, trying to get closer and closer, but once she lifted her papers and began to address them, the pack fell silent.

'Everyone wants stable government,' she began. 'No matter your political persuasion, no matter your gender, your job or your age, we all want our country to run efficiently and sensibly. Over the last seven years, while I have been a member of the Cabinet, and in the years before that when I served in the Shadow Cabinet, I have always done my best to make my department run as efficiently as possible and to do all I could to help those in need. And I will admit that the prospect of becoming prime minister was something I relished because, quite frankly, I've always believed that I could do the job and do it well. But, as you all know, the past few weeks have been very trying for my family and me. We've come under such intense scrutiny – scrutiny that perhaps no politician should ever have to endure – and it's had a dreadful effect on us. And I say this to my fellow party members and parliamentary colleagues: my family matters more to me than any of you do and they always will. So you can take your small-minded bigotry and – excuse my language – shove it where the sun don't shine. I've had to change and it's time for everyone to do the same. And so it is with a heavy heart but a sincere hope for the future that I announce now that I will –'

She stopped suddenly, and I glanced up at her, wondering whether she might have changed her mind. But, no, it wasn't that she was rewriting her speech on the spot. Instead, she was looking past the reporters, past the microphones, past the television cameras and out on to the street beyond.

Standing there was a seventeen-year-old boy wearing jeans and an Arsenal top. He hadn't shaved in a few days and a layer of stubble covered his chin and cheeks. His hair was trimmed short in a buzz cut, like young soldiers usually had when they first joined the army. He was wearing Doc Martens boots and carrying a bag over his shoulder. Everyone turned towards him. I don't think I'd ever seen a boy look so . . . boyish as he did. But he also looked miserable. Almost like a pretend boy. My brother Jason might have looked exactly how we'd all been begging him to look for ages, but for the first time I realized he didn't look like himself – *herself* – at all.

He walked slowly towards the front door, his head down, and the reporters parted as they let him through. When he reached us, Mum and Dad stared at him as if they couldn't quite believe that he'd come home.

'What have you done to yourself?' asked Mum, looking him up and down, her hand reaching up and moving slowly across the top of his head.

'I've gone back to who I used to be,' he said quietly, unable to look any of us in the eye. 'It's what you wanted, isn't it? It'll help you get the job. I don't mind, I swear. I can do this, I promise I can. I'll never talk about it again. I'll stay like this. I'll stay like Jason.'

'After everything you've been through?' asked Mum. 'After everything we've put you through? You'd give it all up for me?'

He nodded.

Mum and Dad simply stared at him and then at each other, and when he caught my eye, all I could do was look down at the ground because I felt so ashamed of my behaviour over recent months and so proud of how brave he had been.

The silence broke then and the reporters began roaring questions at us. 'Jason?' they cried. 'Have you come back for good, Jason? Do you still think you're a girl, Jason?'

'There *is* no Jason,' I shouted at the top of my voice, the first time I had ever spoken to the reporters, and every single one of them went silent as they turned their cameras and microphones in my direction.

None of my family spoke either, but I could feel their eyes on me. I swallowed hard. For the first time in my life, I was visible to the whole world and I wanted to be.

'There *is* no Jason,' I repeated, but more quietly now as I turned to my right and looked up at the person I had loved and idolized my entire life. 'My brother's name is Jessica.'

10

The Top of the Greasy Pole

Until you've lived in 10 Downing Street, you can't imagine what a strange place it is. When my family lived on Rutherford Road, we had four floors and more room than we knew what to do with. Now we live in a small flat with only two bedrooms and two bathrooms, and when my sister comes back from university, as she does every third weekend, we have to share a bedroom, which is totally embarrassing, although we have the most amazing talks, like we used to do when I was a little kid. And every time I walk up or down the stairs I have to stare at portraits and photographs of grumpy-looking men, and two women, who've all held the job that Mum holds now. I suppose they'll put her picture up there too after we've left, although that doesn't seem like it's going to be any time soon as she keeps going up and up in the polls.

At least Bradley is still there to pick me up every morning and drive me to school, and when he drops me at the gates he disappears off to do whatever it is he does before collecting me again later on.

Sometimes, I bring three friends home with me – Jake Tomlin, Alison Beetle and my best friend, David Fugue, because we're all in a band together. Jake's on guitar, Alison's on drums, I'm on keyboards and David is the singer. I have to admit he's really good too. We're called Your Breakfast and we're going to be huge. We thought about calling ourselves You're Breakfast, just to confuse people, but in the end we decided against it. David and I became friends soon after my mother became prime minister. At first, I think he just wanted to feel important, but eventually he told me that he was very sorry for the way he'd treated me ever since we first met. When I asked him why he'd been so mean, he said that he'd been feeling very confused about his own life and had decided to take things out on me, especially after all those rumours started, but that he really regretted it because, actually, he'd always liked me. And then he told me that he'd kissed Jake Tomlin and they were going out with each other and I wasn't to tell anyone, and I haven't said a word, even though it would cause a major scandal and it would be all anyone talked about for weeks.

The civil servants don't like it when we go out to the back garden overlooking Horse Guards Road to play, but whenever anyone complains Mum silences them with a look and that's the end of that. And if you think Mum is bad, then Dad is even worse. Once, when the President of the United States was visiting and he came out to complain about the noise we were making, Dad followed him into the garden and gave him a piece of his mind, saying that if we didn't encourage young people in healthy activities like music, then they'd only go to rack and ruin and turn into mentally deranged lunatics who never read a book and have zero respect for anyone but themselves. The President got very angry at that point and his wig fell off, and when Alison Beetle tried to hand it to him three Secret Service men charged at her and pushed her to the ground. Now, she might only be a sixteen-year-old girl, but because she's a drummer she's actually pretty strong and she started giving it back good to them, so then our own security men had to come running out to separate everyone, and before we knew it there was a diplomatic incident. Later, the President put out a tweet that said:

Hard to watch TV when low IQ kids are playing awful music outside window. Sad!

And despite the Foreign Office begging him not to, Dad tweeted him back saying 'you'. Although he didn't just say 'you', of course, there was a word before the 'you'. And it rhymed with 'duck'.

Mum has been prime minister for two years now and it seems like, in general, people think she's doing a pretty good job. She's made sure to put money into causes she believes in, but she keeps the money back if she thinks that the people administering the money are doing a bad job. Plus, she's been all over the world – to America, Canada, Asia and almost every country in Europe. But she likes Australia the best and, when she took me with her last year for my sixteenth birthday, the Prime Minister of Australia took us to a pub called Fortune of War, the oldest pub in Sydney, and I sat in the back while they were talking about boring politics, and drank seven beers before falling over in a corner. Then I insisted on singing 'Waltzing Matilda' at the top of my voice and had to be carried outside. All her aides tried to stop the press from taking photographs of me throwing up in the gutter, but she told them to go ahead and do what they liked, that I'd be mortified when I woke up and saw pictures of myself in the newspapers the next day and it might teach me a lesson and stop me from doing it again. And, in fairness, when I picked up a copy of the *Sydney Morning Herald* from outside my hotel room door the following morning and saw photographs of myself lying on the ground looking like an idiot, I did feel a bit embarrassed. They were all over the British papers too.

Things between my parents and me are a lot different now to how they used to be. Although Mum is very busy, she makes sure that one night a week and every Sunday afternoon we spend a couple of hours together when I'm supposed to tell her everything that's going on in my life.

'From now on, I can't tell you *everything*,' I told her recently, though, because there's stuff that I definitely can't talk to my mother about. 'Some things are private.'

'All right,' she said, looking a little nervous. 'But don't forget, if there's ever anything you want to talk about – *anything* – then you mustn't be shy about coming to your father or me. There's no problem too big that we wouldn't be here to support you.'

'OK,' I told her. 'But there isn't really anything.' Which is the truth, because everything's fine.

Not long ago, though, I asked her how many years she thought she'd be in the job.

'Another five or six at most,' she said. 'Then it'll be enough. Time to let someone else take over and we can all enjoy our lives. But there are still lots of things I want to achieve. There's no point having a job like this unless you're actually going to do something with it. And I've barely started, Sam. Some day you'll look back and feel proud of your mum.'

'I already am proud of you,' I told her.

It's strange, but it feels like everything has been different since she became prime minister. All those years when she was working her way up the greasy pole she barely seemed to notice that I was even alive but, now that she's got the top job at last, it's like she can't get enough of me. In a way, it's good, but I can't seem to forget how things used to be. Sometimes I want to talk to her about how ignored I felt back then, and how left out, but it doesn't seem like the right time just now. One day, maybe.

I don't feel anger towards her any more, though, just some confusion when I look back at my younger days and wonder why she behaved the way she did. But then

I look back at myself when I was a kid and wonder why I behaved as I did too. We're none of us perfect, I suppose. And, anyway, she's my mum.

Laura Brewster isn't my girlfriend any more, but I still see her a lot because she lives next door, at 11 Downing Street. Mum made her father, Bobby, the Chancellor of the Exchequer, even though he'd tried to stab her in the back. *Keep your friends close*, she told me, *and your enemies closer.* There are a few interconnecting doors between their flat and ours, and Laura and I bump into each all the time.

We never got back together but we became good friends, and if it wasn't for her I wouldn't have met Catherine, my new girlfriend, who I've been with for almost five months now. Catherine is in the same class as Laura at school, and when I met her in the kitchen at Number 11 during the summer I couldn't talk. I mean I literally couldn't talk. I just stared at her and forgot how to make sounds. And I kept staring until she punched me in the arm to snap me out of it, so I tried to make witty and clever remarks but they all came out weird, and I really think she thought that I had something wrong with me. But the next time I saw her I tried again, and this time I managed to speak without making a complete fool of myself. Then there was a disco at school and I asked her to dance and we've been together ever since.

Although recently a new girl called Ayesha started in our school because her family has moved to England from Delhi and she sits next to me in English. She helps me with my reading and stops the words from floating around the page, and we have great conversations about life in India and now I want to go there some day. I really like her, and I think she likes me too, but I'm supposed to be going out with Catherine. I'm not sure what's going to happen, but I feel like there's trouble on the horizon.

Jessica didn't do very well in her A-levels, but perhaps that was to be expected after the difficult time we'd had that year. But she decided to sit them again the following summer, and this time she got the results she needed and moved to Norwich, where she's studying English at university. I go to visit her once or twice a term and stay for the weekend, and we go for long walks around the lake and talk about our lives.

She looks much more like a girl than a boy now because she's taking those special tablets and she doesn't get a beard or moustache any more. Also, although I try not to look, she's definitely getting boobs. And she dresses like a girl and I notice that guys look at her when they pass, because she really looks like a girl now and not like a boy. She seems happy about that, although she tells me that every day is still difficult, and she has counselling and a doctor to help her because she's not sure what lies ahead, except she's sure that she made the right decision. She's playing football again too. She's the only girl on the team, but no one at university seems to care because she's better than most of them anyway.

Whenever I come back down to London after staying with her, I always feel a bit worried for her, even though I know she's living exactly the way she wants to, and I spend the time looking out of the window, watching the scenery go by and thinking about her instead of listening to music or reading.

The last time I came back, I was sitting opposite an elderly lady who was trying to send a message to her daughter to tell her that she'd missed her train and caught the later one instead so she shouldn't come to Liverpool Street too early. Only every time she tried, it wouldn't work, and I could see that she was getting more and more frustrated. I asked her what was wrong and offered to take a look at her phone, but it was really old, and I asked her whether she'd dropped it because I could hear something rattling inside.

'On the platform as I was boarding the train,' she said. 'It just fell out of my hands. Oh dear, do you think you can get it to work again? My daughter will be waiting there with the twins. I don't want her to be standing around for hours unnecessarily.'

'Sorry, I think it's done for,' I said, handing it back. 'But you can text her from mine if you like, as long as you know the number.'

She did, and she typed the message and pressed send, before returning the phone to the home screen. As she handed it back, she paused and looked at the screensaver. It was a picture taken over the weekend of me standing outside the English department, grinning like a maniac.

'Look at you!' said the old woman. 'You don't often see people that happy. And who's that very pretty girl standing next to you? Is that your girlfriend? She looks delighted too. Oh, I can remember looking like that, so excited about life, when I was young!'

I laughed and took the phone back, looking at the picture myself for a couple of moments, recognizing that, yes, the expressions on our faces were cheerful ones. The bad days were over, it seemed.

'No, she's not my girlfriend,' I said, shaking my head. 'Gross! That's my sister. My sister Jessica.'

Acknowledgements

For all their advice and support, many thanks to Naomi Colthurst and all the team at Penguin Random House Children's Books; to Simon Trewin, Eric Simonoff and everyone at WME; to my publishers around the world, who publish my books with such commitment and enthusiasm; and, of course, to my readers. Thank you all.

Afterword

The worst piece of advice anyone can give a writer is to write about what they know. Who wants to do something so limiting? One of the reasons I write is because I want to explore the lives of other people. I find it both interesting and challenging to write about what I *don't* know and to use my writing to learn about a subject, to understand it and to represent it as authentically as possible in order to help others make sense of it too.

In all my books for younger readers, I've written about children who are isolated in some way, whether through the effects of war, grief or abandonment. As my books for adults have grown more personal in nature, so has my writing for young people, and I became interested in exploring how a child would deal with complicated issues of gender and sexuality, not when it's a struggle that *they're* facing, but when the struggle belongs to someone they love.

We all know what it's like to be young and to be desperate to fit in. Anything that singles us out from others can be frightening. It can lead to bullying and isolation. It's hard to stand up for those who are already being victimized because to throw in our lot with them can make us a target too. But if we don't stand up for the oppressed, then one way or another we become the oppressors. If we don't stand side by side with the bullied, then we're complicit in the bullying. So, pick a side. Choose the kind of person you want to be. And be able to live with that decision.

I don't know what it's like to be transgender, but I know what it's like to grow up feeling different to other people and to be frightened about what that difference might mean or the consequences of revealing it to people. When I was Sam's age, I started to realize that I was gay and the idea terrified me. I confided in no one because I didn't think anyone would understand. When I was Jessica's age, I was still in denial and frightened of my friends or family finding out. And then, around the age of twenty, I realized that I would never be happy if I was living a lie and that if people didn't like me for who I was then, quite frankly, they could sod off. So I told people. I told everyone. And life was a million times better when I did because people will often surprise you with just how kind and supportive they can be.

Talking to young transgender people while writing this novel, I was struck by their bravery but, more than that, by their honesty. Here are people who need to live their lives in the most authentic way they can – as themselves, as their true selves – and it takes a lot of guts to do that when society can be unkind to anyone who doesn't fit into its narrow definition of gender. People fear what they don't understand. But the more you educate yourself on a subject, the more you understand that there's nothing to be frightened of.

I hope *My Brother's Name Is Jessica* will enlighten young readers about the extraordinary courage of transgender youth and help them realize that this is just another facet of human nature that can be celebrated.